The Taxi Chronicles

by

S.G. Rogers

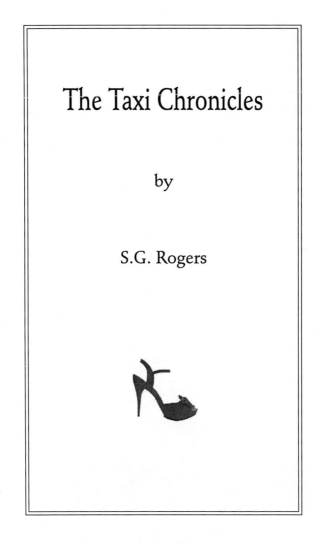

First edition e-book published by Village Green Press LLC

ISBN 9780978863487

If you want to know what is really
happening, ask the taxi driver.

∽

This book is dedicated to
professional drivers everywhere.

Chapter 1

When she shot my front seat, I thought about getting a different job. But it was the passenger side and empty, so I didn't update my resume. And I was surrounded by guys in blue uniforms with guns pointing at my cab. I was inside.

A small-town taxi is a vehicle with built-in entertainment. I should know. My name is Honey Walker. I drive for Cool Rides Cab Company in Northampton, Massachusetts.

Attitude goes with driving a taxi. In this town there are women, men and others who can stop traffic with their attitude and, sometimes, their appearance. We have gender combinations that turn downtown drivers into rubbernecking idiots. Me, I'm the girl who makes the phrase "they all look alike" a reality. When I was a kid and a tomboy, I wanted to look tough. My best friend and I played a lot of cops and robbers so I thought a scar running down my cheek would lend reality to my role as a bad guy. I ended up with a scab that itched like hell for a week. As a teenager I considered a tattoo but the pain factor won out. I remain free of "distinguishing marks." A nose job for me would be to add a few inches and a bump. I personify the term WASP. Blond hair, blue eyes, 5 feet 6 inches tall, yada, yada, yada. It lets me be anonymous when I want to be. Which can be convenient … or not. Right now, it didn't make much difference.

People use taxis for lots of reasons. We get regular calls from the cops telling us not to pick up a guy on whatever street. Contact central immediately if the escapee calls for a ride. This morning's fare hadn't been a prisoner, but she definitely fell into the "shouldn't have" category.

She'd called for a ride to the courthouse. I figured her for a lawyer. Or a thief. She had that arrogant, self-assured walk. Might mean a big tip. She was in front of a hair salon. I should have noticed the salon was next to a bait, tackle and gun shop. She was thin and her face was kind of horsey, but her hair looked freshly styled, with that very in short back, long in front cut. So I just assumed. Hey, hindsight is everything.

She got in. Definitely lawyer. Power clothing, briefcase, nice shoes – really nice shoes – red leather spikes with gold trim. Flashy, but you need to be noticed in a courtroom. I always thought if Marcia Clark had owned a better wardrobe, O.J. would have been in the slammer a lot sooner.

"So where'd you get the shoes?" I asked, figuring she'd want to share sources. She must be a shoe girl. Look at what she was wearing.

"Just drive," she snapped.

"Yeah, okay," I grumbled. What kind of woman wears shoes like that and won't talk about them?

We pulled up to the courthouse. "Wait for me," she ordered.

"There's a 10-dollar wait fee."

"Fine." She stalked off up the sidewalk, her heels drumming like Charlie Watts playing Honky Tonk Women.

I pulled into the no-parking zone, down-buttoned the windows to let in a breeze and turned off the engine. I adjusted the band in my excessively curly hair. With the air conditioner off, it was about 90 in the sun. If the police noticed me before she came out, I could smile and hope my melting mascara hadn't made me look like a terrorist raccoon. Then I'd move to a legal spot.

Ten minutes later she flew out the side exit five feet from where I'd parked. "Drive," she screamed and slammed into the backseat.

Rule one of taxi driving: Never drive when someone is yelling at you. Then I caught the black metal shape of a gun in my peripheral vision. I felt something small, round and cold against my neck. I had never had a gun actually touch me.

I yanked the steering wheel around and mashed my foot to the floor. The taxi leaped forward. Right into the police car in front of me. The impact threw my passenger back against the seat. The gun went flying, landed with a thump, and shot the front passenger seat.

"Shit!" I threw it into reverse, twisting the wheel the other direction. I hadn't noticed the car behind me. A blue wave of cops flooded out of the courthouse and surrounded the taxi. They had guns, big guns. And they were all pointed at me.

7

"Oops," I whispered and slid down the seat.

All four doors to my car opened at the same time and cop hands grabbed anything they could get. That would be me, my fare, and her gun. Which they handled with a lot more care than they handled us. We were cuffed, stuffed and driven over to the police station in the injured cop car. My fare maintained a stony silence while I stammered and stuttered about my innocence.

In 30 seconds, we pulled up to the police station. Northampton is not a big town. But there were probably rules about how to safely transport dangerous prisoners. Like one of us might try to escape with at least a million cops surrounding us. So there I was in handcuffs. I was pretty sure I had a lawyer sitting next to me, but she was as mute as a dead fish. They hauled us out and dragged us inside.

Northampton is a city with a funky outlook and matching location. Right off the interstate, it's a prime setting for everything from gourmet eating and till-you-drop shopping to drug running and money laundering. As it's the county seat, there's a courthouse, which is convenient for the drug runners and money launderers. Since the police force, the local legal establishment and the whole legal system at least partly depend on the existence of the dirty money the criminal activities generate, it all forms a nice circular economic interdependence with the courthouse at its center.

The front half of this historic building is made up of huge gray stone blocks and dates back to the 1800s. The rear end new addition looks like an 18-wheeler hauled in a prefab, postmodern trailer park. One local critic called it an architectural debauchery.

The population is a mix of sane and crazy, rich and homeless, ultra-conservative and flaming liberal, and lots of other, more mysterious lifestyles. Our mayor of the moment is liberal. Our mayor for the previous 8 years was liberal, gay and a woman. We are surrounded by institutions of higher learning. We also have one of the oldest agricultural county fairs in the U.S.; once a year the fairgrounds fill up with farmers and 4-H kids hauling cows, horses, ducks and chickens. They have a demolition derby that wipes out about 50 cars.

I don't know if the mayor has ever been to the county fair. I've been there enough to make myself sick on deep-fried everything. One of our city councilors looks like King Kong and dresses like Marilyn Monroe. Northampton wears the sophisticated glamour of a big city, but the functional underwear of its agricultural, blue-collar origins sometimes rides up its butt crack and shows over the top of the tailored Armani slacks. It's a tolerant dish with a side order of perversity. But cops are cops everywhere, and none of them like to see anyone except them using guns.

Half an hour after a bullet drilled my passenger seat, I was in interrogation thinking that even with its odd construction, the courthouse seemed dignified compared with the cop house which has been called one of the worst-looking organizational disasters in the city's history. Outside, it's a flat-topped, utilitarian brick building. Inside, it's a rat maze. Trying to find a way out would be time-consuming and pointless. The cops know where they are, and they know where you are. They are busy putting up a new building to house the boys in blue, but the old one is still in use and still feels like a rat maze.

I was somewhere deep in the maze. The guy questioning me was so overweight and genial it was hard to feel intimidated.

"Aiding and abetting!" he said. "And destroying city property. And attempted departure from the scene."

"Hey, I had a gun in my face. I saved you guys a high-speed chase down Main Street. How was I supposed to know what my fare was up to?"

More realistically, I'd had a gun in my back and no way to get out of the parking space without a tank.

This guy was a sergeant. A gun in the courthouse should merit someone higher up. They were probably deciding who got the short straw and had to sort out my part in the fiasco.

After 10 minutes of scowling and pacing, my interviewer was replaced by Lieutenant Jon Stevens. I know Jon. I call him Jon Jon because he's so boyishly cute. Movie-star good looks, tight buns and a fabulous smile. He wasn't smiling now. But it was hard for me to keep my heart rate from picking up a little when he came in.

"You still drive for Cool Rides, huh?" He stood over me. I wasn't intimidated by his scowl. I did have to suppress the urge to reach out and touch him, since my face was just below belt level.

"Was that a question? Or are you introducing me?" I snapped.

His bright blue eyes stared at me for so long that I looked down to make sure my shirt was buttoned and I didn't have any blood dripping down my front.

"What?" I jutted my chin forward defiantly.

"Did you know the woman?"

"Lady Red Shoes?"

"No," he said. "The woman in pink lace underwear. Who did you think I meant?"

The image of pink lace underwear and Lieutenant Jon Jon was pretty appealing. A straight woman's wet dream.

"She was a fare," I told him. "And, speaking of fares, I didn't get paid. And I didn't get my wait charge. And the boss is going to be so pissed when he sees the dent in the car. And the other cars are going to file insurance claims." I was beginning to wail.

"Jesus Christ, spare me. We got a guy in the hospital getting a bullet out of his butt and his crazy-lady lawyer-wife who put it there is in holding. I don't give a rat's ass about your cash flow." He turned away but was still standing with his ass at eye level. I stifled the urge to stroke it. He looked down at his feet. My gaze followed, but there was nothing there except his size 10s. He looked at the ceiling. I looked at the ceiling. Nothing there either.

He stalked over to the door, knocked once and said to the sergeant, "Cut her loose."

I dragged through the warren of the cop house. I didn't want to face my boss. I did want to know the story on the lady lawyer. I wanted to collect my fare and, mostly, I wanted to know where she got those shoes.

My curiosity sometimes gets me into trouble. So I figured if I dealt with my boss first, I could come back to the holding cells later and visit the shoes. I called in and talked fast. I wanted to explain the situation before he started yelling.

"How bad?" I could feel his seething over the cell phone. Still, I decided it was better to tell him about the dent rather than show up pretending I hadn't noticed it. And that I hadn't spent the last hour running fares.

"We just got a scratch. And the cop car isn't too horrible. The civilian car is kind of dented."

"If the cab can be driven, get your ass back here." The boss didn't ask whether I was hurt, or even alive.

I flipped the phone closed and started the car. It was late in the morning and I'd probably missed a half a day's worth of pickups, as well as my morning caffeine and sugar fix. I sighed and headed back to the office.

The whole crew was standing out front when I drove up. The Cool Rides Company is sort of like that TV show from the '70s with Judd Hirsch and Danny DeVito. Except the cars are more like The Italian Job. We don't have Mini Coopers, but the Scion XB has personality. Think a chopped British taxicab. Or a Mini on steroids. There were five of them lined up in front of the office window. All in perfect clean condition, each one a different color. They had interesting graphics running down their sides and around their backs and cute names printed on the fenders. My personal favorite was the flame job with yellow taxi checkerboard inside the flames. Each one had lettering that said "Cool Rides, the Best Ride Ever" across the doors. They were all freshly washed, waxed, and vacuumed. And now there was mine. The dented fenders would have fit in fine with any other cab company. At Cool Rides, it looked like it had been through a junkyard slalom. I didn't mention the bullet hole in the seat. The cops had confiscated the gun and the bullet hole hardly showed.

The boss avoided looking directly at the car. I knew he wanted to kick my ass around the parking lot. But Willie has the personality of a golden retriever trying to pass as a rottweiler. His thick, curly white hair falls in uncontrolled splendor, and his gray eyes are kind. He's not the hard-ass he thinks he should be.

Andrew, one of the other drivers, stepped forward as I pulled to a stop.

"Wow! Hey, boss, do ya think the car is embarrassed? It kinda hurts to look at it." He fidgeted and danced around the car. "Maybe we should hide it around back." He shuffled up the other side and almost stopped in front of me. He couldn't actually stand still, but he gave it his best effort, drumming a loose finger on his leg, tapping a free toe, bobbing his head to music I could never hear. Being around Andrew was like being around a small explosive device. He jittered away, bouncing like an overheated electron, polishing a nonexistent spot on one of the cars with his shirttail.

Mona, the dispatcher, gave me a look that could have leveled Muhammad's mountain. I still can't get used to her soft sultry voice coming out of a 5-foot-2-inch body as wide as a linebacker's. She resembles the Rottweiler her boss wants to be and protects him like one. Sometimes we call her Moanin' Lisa or just Moanin'. Her dark eyes told me not to mess with the Boss. He was in a pile of hurt. I wanted to say "hey, me too," but I kept my mouth shut.

"So whad she do?" Andrew wanted to know. The word from the courthouse had gotten back to the office before I did.

"She shot her husband. In the court room ... and in the buttocks." I glanced at Willie to see if I was getting sympathy. "And caused general mayhem." I paused. "While I was waiting for her." Not even a flicker of compassion from Willie.

"Wow, how'd she get a gun past the checkpoint?" Andrew was leaning over rubbing the dent in the front fender while his feet beat a little pattern on the ground.

"She's a lawyer. They don't always search them." I'm a good a judge of clothing, and her suit had lawyer written all over it. Too bad I wasn't as good a judge of human character. My front seat might not have a bullet hole in it.

∽

Since I didn't get any sympathy at Cool Rides, I decided to see how hard it would be to see Lady Red Shoes. Maybe if I collected the fare and wait fee, Willie would forgive my unavoidable accident. And what the hell was this woman doing shooting someone in the butt, in the courthouse, in broad daylight?

Andrew, also our resident body man, had taken my car into the garage to assess the damage, so I walked to the police station only to find that my favorite red shoes had been released on bail. Her husband refused to press charges, and that lowered the violation – and thus the bail – significantly. The cops were left with illegal discharge of a firearm. She had a permit for it. Being a lawyer, I'm sure she knew how to get out of jail faster than a Monopoly card. I might have to find my own pair of red spikes and then wear them into the police station just to see how Jon Jon would react. Maybe with some pink lace undies.

As I was walking up Main Street, my cell phone buzzed. The only cell phone I carry is the one Cool Rides issues to all its drivers. So I knew this was work-related, hopefully a fare. That meant the boss was willing to let me drive again.

I got to the garage and Mona handed me a slip with name, address and phone number.

"Another ride to the courthouse. Take the same cab. The boss said it's drivable, so it might as well be you that drives it. He figures to limit the damage to one vehicle." Mona gave me a look that said "you're stupid" all over it.

"Hey, none of it was my fault. You can even ask Lieutenant Jon Jon. He's the one who cut me loose."

"You got a private audience with Lieutenant Jon Jon?" Mona's expression changed to "I'm jealous."

"Details when you get back."

"What's the story on this fare? Much as I like Jon Jon, I don't think I want to be hauled in front of him again quite this soon. He was a tad grouchy about my first appearance."

"She has a tracking bracelet and she's wearing it, so they know she's coming. Pickup is Hamp Heights."

I groaned. "A tracking bracelet? Why? And why are you giving her to me?"

"Everyone else is out."

I looked out the window. She was right. My car had been moved back out of the garage. It was alone in the lot. Slightly smushed but still cute.

"Okay." I shuffled out the door, head hanging.

"Pitiful doesn't look good on you," Mona yelled after me. She was right. It was a lousy fashion statement.

Hamp Heights is Northampton's version of a housing project. It started as low-income but luxurious apartments in the '70s. It hasn't aged well. It's of the dead toy, dead plants, lots of trash school of landscaping. Unfortunately, the buildings are brick and solid enough to withstand any destructive force, natural or man-made. They will stand forever, or until a new generation of urban planners bulldozes them into a pile of rubble. Then they will be replaced by whatever the current politically correct housing might be. And the cycle will start over.

I've never had a problem with any of the fares I pick up there, but they don't tip and they always keep me waiting while they dig up enough change to pay the eight-dollar fee. I stopped at the apartment number on my fare slip. A car of undetermined make and color was on four cement blocks next to the curb. It had no wheels, no doors and no hood. There was half a child's bike lying by the step. One side was sort of flat. Some brown flowers sprawled next to it. The screen door hung by one hinge.

The person who slammed it open was 6 feet of mocha-brown WOMAN in 2 feet of sequined red spandex. The door flew off its remaining hinge and into the dead land-scape. Clattering down the steps in her 4-inch black and silver spike heels my fare yanked open the car door before I could get out and open it for her.

The Scion XB is a roomy automobile for its size. I was more worried about the shocks grounding out than about fitting her in the backseat. She wedged in, ducking her head to fit. I didn't mention the seat belt issue. We aren't supposed to go anywhere with a passenger until they fasten it. I decided not to argue with someone who had just ripped a screen door out of a brick wall. Then I noticed the tracking bracelet. Not a good fashion statement unless you're a card-carrying member of the criminal sisterhood, and it did not go with her spiky, silver-sequined shoes. But her fingernails did. They were red and silver and had to be 2 inches long and curved like the talons of the raptors in Jurassic Park.

"Nice nails." I said.

"Yeah, you gotta be real careful pickin' your nose." She slumped back in the seat. Okay, not good woman-friend material. I could deal with that. Those fingernails must be good for something. I just couldn't think what.

When we got to the courthouse, my favorite Lieutenant was waiting at the entrance. I hopped out of the cab and opened the door. She took her time getting out of the car, so I offered my hand to speed things up.

"Hey, time is money, ma'am," I grumbled.

She grabbed my hand and gave a sharp yank. Since she outweighed me by about 50 pounds, I landed face-first in her lap with my nose buried in her crotch. Eek! Hastily pushing myself backward and out the door, I turned in time to see Jon trying to suppress a grin.

"Fine." I scowled at him. "A gentleman would give us a hand here."

He stepped forward, smiling broadly, and offered his hand. She exited gracefully, batting mascara coated eyelashes.

"Pick her up in an hour." Jon leaned over and flipped a curl of hair out of my face. My heart fluttered a few beats.

∽

Yeah. Jon and I have history. When I first came to Northampton, I was basically homeless. But I was young and on an adventure. When I turned 17, my parents gave me a road map for my post-high school life. Three months traveling in Europe, on to four years of college, where I would have a four-point GPA, and find a respectable profession and a more respectable husband. At this point, my parents thought their child-rearing job would be over. I did the travel thing. I did the college thing for a few months. No profession inspired and no husband appeared, so at the mature age of almost 18 I developed my own plan. It excluded the boredom of the classroom. I hitchhiked from Chicago to New York and north to Massachusetts. I landed in Northampton because it was right off the interstate and I needed a bathroom break.

I was spending nights on park benches and days looking for work. Jon found me on my bench one night when he was walking patrol. He suggested that it wasn't safe for a woman to spend nights on benches, even in Northampton. I suggested that it was none of his business where I spent my nights. He started lecturing me on lifestyle, and I started telling him what I thought of his profession. I think I used the word pig a few times. I might have used a few more inflammatory words as well. And maybe I poked him in the ribs, or maybe it was more than a poke. Jon used his handcuffs and I spent the night in protective custody. I yelled about lack of a charge, and he calmly replied about assault on an officer and my personal safety. I told him that it would be a hell of lot more obvious if I assaulted him. And the only thing I wasn't safe from was him. Jon was young, serious and idealistic. I was young, rebellious and a little crazy. I couldn't believe he was arresting me. In retrospect, I still can't believe he arrested me. What I learned was that there is no sound quite like the slamming of a cell door.

After my night in jail, he delivered me to Willie at the Cool Rides garage and told him I needed a job. I told him I could handle my own life, thank you very much. I've been with Cool Rides ever since. Everyone on the force knows about Jon hosting my overnight in the jail. One of my female cop friends told me that Jon also spent that night at the holding cells. Mostly checking up on me every half-hour or so. It was a rocky beginning to a relationship that has since mostly consisted of circling each other like dogs with our hackles up. I stay pretty busy with my job, and I guess he does, too. Somehow we haven't crossed paths socially or professionally again, thank God. We've both grown up some in five years. Maybe Jon more than me.

Since that first encounter, Jon has used his brains to work his way up the promotional ladder to lieutenant. I used my college fund to buy into Cool Rides Taxi Company. We keep an eye on each other without much close contact.

Jon sees life as a puzzle. Which is probably why he's a good cop. I see life as my personal entertainment. I'm never disappointed. But I want to be in charge of my life. I keep my distance from Jon because I'm not sure I could handle whatever it is he might offer. He's an in-control kind of guy and I'm an out-of-control kind of woman. But that doesn't mean I'm not tempted.

My dream is to own the taxi company when Willy retires. My college fund wasn't close to enough to get more than 10 percent, and I actually asked a few banker friends what they thought of the loan possibility. They laughed for longer than I thought was polite. A month after I had talked to them, I was sitting uptown next to the taxi sipping my five-dollar oversize, excessively whipped mocha. Two guys who looked like they had just walked off the set of Godfather V approached me.

"So, we hear you wanna buy a taxi company." He sounded like he looked.

"Huh?" I said with all the intelligence I could muster.

"The Cool Rides Cab Company. We could help you buy it. We hear you might need some cash to make the deal."

"Who are you?"

"We're like, ah … bankers. We make loans."

"What bank do you work for?"

"You wouldn't know it. It's from some distance away. Not your concern. We just give you money. You do us a few favors. Ya know?"

"I don't know. And any loans I get need to have a contract attached to them. Who are you?" I smiled sweetly and played as dumb as I felt.

The two guys left. I never saw them again, but I wondered if I had let something go by me that I should have listened to.

Right now, I zipped back to Cool Rides. Mona handed me a call slip.

"You got two short hauls. Fit them in before you go back to the courthouse."

"Yes, ma'am." I trotted back out the door. My first pickup was a man who needed to get his car from the impound lot. We get a lot of business from the impound lot. This guy's car had been towed when he was stopped by the police for erratic driving. He took out an entire row of newspaper vending boxes before snapping off a fire hydrant. The result was instant papier-mâché.

"Ha, they thought I was drunk. I was just making sure my letter to the editor about those idiot newspaper boxes made the front page." It did. The picture was of the rup- tured fire hydrant with a newspaper, opened to the editorial page, draped over it. The caption read, "Local man makes editorial statement." His "statement" had only cost him $200 in towing fees and who knows how much in damage to the hydrant and the ticket for driving to endanger. And then there was the cab fare. The newspaper wasn't press- ing charges. They probably sold a thousand more papers.

I dropped him at the impound lot. About all that could be said about his car was that it was still drivable. It had been a rusted-out boat before he mowed down the first amendment. Now it had paint from the news boxes added to the rust. I collected my eight-dollar fare and watched him limp to his car. It started and thumped out of the lot. The front wheel tilted a bit, but he took off with a screech in one direction and I motored sedately in the other. I didn't have far to go. The second short haul was parked at the other end of the impound lot.

This idiot had parked his car in a handicapped space and gone into the first bar he found, which was the width of the sidewalk away. He staggered out an hour later and accidentally "became unconscious" on the backseat of his car. When he woke up he was still in the car, in the impound lot, with no money, having spent it all on booze. He smelled like the floor of an overused bathroom in an overused bar. Breathing through my mouth, I drove him home with all the windows open and the air conditioner on high. His wife screamed that I should have brought home the car and left him impounded. But she paid, no tip.

The impound pickups are mostly idiots, but they're our idiots and the Cool Rides staff treats them with the respect they deserve.

An hour later, I swung back around to the courthouse. Lieutenant Jon and my glittering fare were waiting. He handed me $16 and helped Madam Amazon into the car. No tip. Who did he think was going to pay my rent? How could I buy those shoes I'd wear to walk all over him? Do I seem preoccupied with tips? That's what pays the rent, and the fun money.

"Okay, lady, let's hustle," she said. "I got appointments to keep." I was pretty sure I knew what appointments the spandex wonder needed to keep. But I had to drive, so I wasn't wasting time passing judgment. Everybody's life is her own.

I zipped off in the direction of Hampshire Heights. It was an easy drive with no back streets to negotiate. It was built close to a major highway for easy access. And because no developer would ever want to put luxury houses in that location. About halfway there, I heard the sound of a siren coming up fast behind me. I rearviewed it and realized it was an unmarked police car, very close to my rear bumper. The siren blasted, the cop bubble flashed and his headlights were blinking. I pulled over. If I had been speeding it couldn't have been more than five miles over. I plastered a smile on my face, prepared to bat my eyelashes and decided to blame my fare. "Oh, officer, I just was so upset by the funny bracelet she's wearing, I was completely distracted," … bat, bat, bat. Then I remembered that when she'd come out of the courthouse, the bracelet had been removed.

I lowered my window and there was Jon Jon. What had a lieutenant done to pull traffic duty? I didn't know the punishment routine in the Northampton Police Department, but this seemed a bit extreme.

He knelt by my window and looked over to check on my passenger.

"God, I'm glad I caught up with you, both of you." He looked relieved. Relieved?

"What's going on?" My plastered smile faded. My eyes closed and I tipped my head back against the seat. "I know I wasn't speeding very much."

Jon had ignored my fluttering eyelashes, so I figured either I was off my game or something serious was happening.

"There's been a shooting at the Heights," he said in a voice low enough that my backseat passenger couldn't hear. "Stay behind me and pull in when I stop."

Chapter 2

I obediently did as instructed. Rare for me, but Jon's cop face was in "don't ask and I won't tell anyway" mode.

"What? What's goin' on now? I shudda' told you not ta speed. If we get a ticket, I ain't payin'. That's your fault."

This from the lady with the full appointment book. I nodded and kept my mouth shut.

When we arrived at the Heights, police cars were scattered randomly around the parking area. Yellow crime-scene tape circled the small dirt yard, enclosing trash, abandoned toys and other mysterious objects. An ambulance was backed up to the only apartment without a screen door. A metal gurney was being rolled out. My lady of the bracelet shrieked something indecipherable and launched herself out the car's back door. I shook my head to clear my ears. She had the lungs of a Hollywood screamer.

One of the uniforms ran over and tried to keep her outside the police tape. It was like stopping a charging buffalo.

She made it as far as the sheet-draped gurney. Holding off the police officer with one hand, she whipped the covering off the body with the other. With a yelp of anger, she grabbed the dead guy by the throat and lifted him, one-handed, off the metal slab.

"You good-for-nothin' cocksucker! What've you done now? What'm I gonna do now? Huh?" She threw the body to the ground and marched back to my car. Why couldn't she march to someone else's car? I noticed that the police ranks parted to give her easy access to my taxi.

"Take me back downtown," she demanded.

I looked over to the nearest police officer and lifted my hands in a "what now?" gesture. He trotted over to where Jon and several officers were watching the EMTs reload the body onto the gurney. Jon glanced over as the officer waved his hand in my direction. He sighed and hung his head in a frustrated way. Hey, I thought, I didn't do any of this.

He walked over and leaned down by my window.

"I got nothing to hold her on. Take her where she wants to go. But," – he pointed at her – "don't go far. I will want to talk to you."

My spandex Wonder Woman slumped in the backseat and scowled at Jon. Her middle finger did something I hoped Jon didn't see.

Curiosity wasn't going to get the better of me here. I like to know what's going on, but I draw the line at dead people. I floored it, ready to drop my very pissed-off passenger anywhere, fast.

She directed me to an ornate Victorian house in the center of town that had two signs in front of it. One was for a dentist. The other said "Susan Young, Attorney at Law" in gold letters across a black background. Classy sign. My passenger might need someone with class. I wasn't sure why she needed a lawyer, but some guidance with her wardrobe might help her stay out of trouble.

I didn't do the assist-her-out-of-the-car thing this time. I wasn't going to land in dark places again. As my fare fumbled with the door, who should walk up to the house, briefcase in hand, but Lady Red Shoes. Didn't shooting someone in the courthouse constitute grounds for being locked up or at least for not being allowed to practice law? How about stiffing a cabdriver? That was definitely cause for disbarment. I jumped out of my cab and got to her before the Amazon could.

"Hi, remember me?" I stood between her and the building and got up close and personal. Nothing is more personal to a cabdriver than being stiffed for a fare. This woman was a lawyer and she owed me money. She was at the top of my shit list.

Amazon was approaching from behind. We had her cornered. The only question was which one of us wanted her more. It was the principle more than the $18 she owed me. Cabbies can't afford to let the world think they can be taken advantage of. I wanted that fare. I didn't know what Amazon might want, other than a new ankle bracelet.

Lady Red Shoes looked over her shoulder and saw the Amazon closing in from behind. She turned back to me and realized I was blocking her way.

"You owe me, lady."

Amazon crowded closer. "I got a problem, too."

"If both of you would step into my office, I'm sure we can settle this," she replied with enough dignity to take over the throne of England. She was dressed in a dark pantsuit and looked lawyerlike and intimidating. She had the posture thing down: arrogant, aggressive, clenching the briefcase like it was a permanent part of her body. I always have trouble figuring out what to do with my hands, which are usually out, upturned, asking for money. I stuffed them into my pockets and followed her into the building. The only thing I liked about her so far was the chutzpah it took to walk into a courthouse and unload a bullet into someone's rear end. Besides, it was creepy that Amazon, who had recently dealt with a body full of bullet holes, was meeting with a woman who had just drilled bullet holes into her husband's body. I decided to get my fare money and not worry about Amazon and Susan Young.

We entered the waiting room that she shared with the dentist. The wall to the left held framed degrees from various medical schools and something that claimed that Eduardo Kosoloski was allowed to practice dentistry in the state of Massachusetts. The opposite wall gave the right to practice law to Susan Young. If your dentist screwed up, you could cross the room and file a malpractice suit. The walls were soothing pastel greens and peaches. We headed through a door on the right. The paint scheme was the same inside the office. Maybe Home Depot had a sale on psychologically relaxing paint colors.

The concept didn't seem to work on Amazon. She paced and fidgeted and muttered. I couldn't hear every-thing, but the gist of it was that her stupid dog of a husband and, by the way, her pimp and major source of income had fucked up again. My needs seemed trivial by comparison. I had a pissed-off boss and a short fare till. She had a dead body in her life.

I stuck out my hand, palm up, to Susan Young. "I believe you owe me for a fare. And a wait fee."

She opened her oversize bag and pulled out a set of keys. Then she pulled out a notebook, several hardcover law books and a trashy paperback.

"Oh, fuck," she said and emptied her purse onto the nearest chair. A wallet flopped out. And some pepper spray and a set of brass knuckles and a gun. Don't they take those away after you shoot someone?

A piece of paper fluttered to the floor from the pile of purse detritus. I glanced down. It wasn't a grocery list. It was a list of taxi companies from the area, written in careful block letters. Cool Rides was highlighted in yellow, with three checkmarks next to it. If she liked us best, I didn't return the sentiment.

"How much do I owe you?" She snatched the taxi list off the floor and stuffed it back in her purse.

"Are you giving me danger compensation? How 'bout material damages? Emotional distress? To both me and my boss. He gets very emotional about the cars. And I haven't told him about the bullet hole yet."

"Look, I'm really sorry about that stuff at the courthouse. I got crazy when I heard that my husband had surfaced. I needed to make a clear statement about how I felt." Her defiant stance didn't back up the apology.

"Oh, you did that really well. Next time don't take a taxi to do it. Walk! It's good for your health. And mine." I huffed a bit. "Eighteen dollars. And you can take us off that list."

She looked at me with an odd expression, something between anger and guilt. She should have felt guilty. She tried to burn a taxi driver. And she shot her husband.

"That's what you owe me. Fare plus wait fee."

"Right." Her attention had shifted to Amazon, who was becoming increasingly agitated. Susan Young, attorney at law, gave me a 20-dollar bill.

"Keep it," she said.

"Thanks." I shuffled toward the door. I had my money, but my curiosity was gaining ground. What did Amazon want with a lawyer? And what did she know about the dead body? And who was the dead body? And ... I pulled a wallet out of my bag, leaned against the doorjamb and stuffed in the 20. I was just short of being rude when Susan turned and asked if I needed anything more.

"No." I turned to Amazon. "You gonna need a ride home?"

She slumped into one of the customer chairs. The chair groaned and Amazon sniffled. She looked like a stray puppy, a very large stray puppy.

"I guess. I'm not sure I can go back there." She whimpered a little. I had just seen her throw a body to the ground one-handed, and now she was whimpering. It was a little strange.

I sighed. I knew what it was like to be alone, but I'd been lucky. Willie had taken me under his wing, stuck me in a taxi, handed me an address and told me to drive. I'd considered him an angel of major proportions when he let me sleep on the couch in the office. For the first week of my employment, I lived off stale bread and a jar of mayonnaise that some previous driver had left in the office fridge. I don't recommend it as a long-term diet. The reality was that Willie was desperate for drivers. I had a valid driver's license and no felony convictions. Turned out I was good at it.

I sank onto the chair next to Amazon. Susan sat opposite us. That was a good sign. A lawyer's office usually doesn't promote comfort and sympathy. It keeps the person behind the desk in charge of the situation. Amazon didn't need any more intimidation. She had been flying on anger since the dead body. Now that her adrenaline had evaporated, she looked worried and scared.

Susan leaned toward Amazon. She had an almost-sympathetic expression. I realized Susan and Amazon knew each other. It wasn't a social relationship.

"What brings you here, Belle?"

Belle? I looked at Amazon. I had trouble making the name fit.

Belle sniffed. She pulled herself up straight and raised her chin. A queen. I was impressed and reassessed my opinion. She could have class, even in spandex glitter.

"Horace is dead," she said without any of the anger she'd had when she confronted dead Horace.

"What!?" Susan slid off her chair and sat on the other side of Belle. "Oh, Belle, I'm so sorry."

Belle put her hand over Susan's. "Oh, he was never much to me but a pimp. I didn't waste any like on him. So don't you."

Susan sat back. "You didn't kill him, did you?" She glanced at me. "Do we need some privacy?"

Belle smiled sadly. "Naw. Not that there weren't times that I wanted to. But I've got an alibi that even the cops won't break. I was in court. Anyway, I heard a few of the cops talking about that Scarpelli guy out of Springfield, from the crime family, and that scared me. I wonder if I need someplace to stay for a while. I thought you might have someplace you send clients."

I stared at her. She was still using inner-city slang, but the accent was straight out of the British upper class. How weird was that? My native tongue crossed with the Queen's English.

The only thing I was pretty sure of was her profession. She was a prostitute. Horace was her pimp as well as her husband. And who the hell was Scarpelli? Susan had looked startled at the mention of his name.

Belle continued. "I'm not particularly sad to see him gone. He was a mean fucker. The only reason he didn't whack me around's that I'm big. And he wasn't." The refined accent remained. Maybe it was her first language.

Maybe Susan was the friend Belle needed, but lawyers could be your best friend until the law hauled you away and locked you up forever. Then they would be on to their next best friend.

Susan looked intently at Belle. "What did the police say about Scarpelli?"

"Not much." Belle rose and started pacing around the office. She walked with a new grace. No more stomping, striding or slouching. Her posture said, "I'm in charge of myself." Regal. Okay, African Queen, I thought. Either way, no one would mess with her.

"What worries me is who did kill Horace. I need more information, and the police will be as tight as their sphincters about giving me anything. Horace knew the Scarpellis, but I never met any of them personally. If someone is gunning for me, I want to know. And I have to find someplace to stay." That was when she turned to me.

"No." I blurted. "I don't even know you. One minute you're a pissed-off Amazon and the next you're a British … princess."

"Ah," she said. "The accent? I'm bilingual."

Maybe bipolar too, I thought. Did I want to be roomies with a pissed-off royal hooker possibly being stalked by a deranged killer? The police did have a body and they might want to know why it was a dead one. My apartment only had one bed. And a fold-out sofa.

Susan looked at me. "It would only be for a few days. Until I can find out what the police know and what kind of problems Belle has. I'm her attorney, so her location is privileged. We would be the only ones who know where she is."

Belle looked at me speculatively. "Who would think I'd be staying with my taxi driver? And I could pay you some rent money." Her gaze traveled down to my sneaker-clad feet. "Enough for a new pair of shoes."

I was thinking about how to say no when my cell phone rang. When had I become her taxi driver? I did need some new shoes, and she probably knew where to get them.

"Cool Rides, Honey Walker." I answered in my most professional voice.

"You got an airport," Mona purred into the phone. "Pick up at Smith's Funeral Home ASAP. She's a special consideration."

"I'm on it." I answered loud enough so both Susan and Belle could hear and understand that I had a job to do.

"Just a few days," Susan said. She put her hand on my shoulder. "We would both owe you."

I could see that having a lawyer indebted to me might be helpful in future life experiences. But a prostitute? Why would I want that? Of course, she did have fabulous taste in shoes and probably a few sources for them that I had never heard of.

I needed to get my airport fare. "Okay." Crap. I seemed to be doing a lot of blurting lately. I needed to slow down. "Just stay here until I get back from this fare. It should be about two hours." Special consideration meant extra time.

"Thank you," Belle said with the grace of royalty.

I headed out to the car, wondering what I had gotten myself into. Maybe they would figure out some other arrangement by the time I got back. Belle was kind of an interesting person. Having some female friends would be nice. Whatever it was, I was rationalizing myself into the middle of it. I could talk myself out of it while I did the airport run.

I zipped over to the funeral home. The elderly woman sitting by the door was short and slightly plump with curly white hair. She wore an old-lady big print dress and cross trainers on her feet. A cardboard box sat next to her. The funeral-home director was standing behind her. She looked pretty happy with the world and was ignoring him completely.

I hopped out of the cab and grabbed her box. The funeral-home director melted away.

"Whoa!" I said. "What's in here?" The box was small and very heavy.

"Oh, that's my dearly departed husband. And a right big one he was, too." She smiled beatifically. "Do you need some assistance? I was always able to move him by myself. Of course, I never tried doing it with anyone helping. That would be a threesome, wouldn't it?" She beamed at me.

"We're spreading his ashes tomorrow." She settled into the front seat.

"I think I can handle it. Do you want him in the backseat?"

"No, no. I do believe I'd prefer him right here on my lap. That will be a nice reversal of position, won't it?"

"Umm ..." I fastened her seat belt and eased her husband on top of her. She seemed oddly cheerful about the purpose of her trip.

When we got to the airport, I parked in short-term, helped the widow into the shuttle, and heaved the box onto the rack. It settled like a sandbag. I hoped Granddad was well wrapped. With a special-consideration fare, we accompany the passenger into the terminal and see them to security.

The shuttle driver helped Granny off at the terminal and got her settled into a wheelchair. I thanked God for wheelchairs as I staggered back from the shuttle with the box of Grandpa. I put it on Granny's lap, slung my handbag over my shoulder and we were off toward the long line at check-in. The airport was crowded. Security was tight but not restrictive. I could take my fare as far as the checkpoint. An airline employee would take over from there.

"Oh, what a cute little dog." Granny noticed the drug-sniffing beagle that was pacing the walkway with its handler. As we passed it, I heard the dog sneeze. And sneeze. And sneeze. I turned around and noticed a thin gray trail between Grandma, Granddad and the dog. The dog was following the trail. I leaned over and pushed the torn corner back into the box. I dug in my oversize bag while I picked up the pace to get to the wheelchair line. I came up with the standard solution to everything. Duct tape. I tore off a piece, slapped it on Granddad's escape hole and took off in a hurry. The dog stopped sneezing, threw back his head and howled.

"What the hell?" His handler stared at the trail of ash that ended in the middle of the walkway, a good 20 feet from us. I was trying not to watch the beagle when I noticed the ride around vacuum making its hourly sweep of the main concourse. It rumbled from one end of the terminal to the other, making a graceful arc at the far end to turn back and follow our trail past the cute beagle and the hordes of people waiting at security. It roared by, sucking up dust and stray bits of human remains that had inadvertently been scattered on the wall-to-wall carpet. Pieces of Grandpa were whisked away with dust and grit from around the world.

"Is something wrong?" Granny noticed me staring at the giant vacuum.

"Oh, no. I just wonder how they keep this place clean. With so many people and all." A little bit of Granddad wouldn't make it to his final resting place. Most of him would be spread to the wind. And the wind would spread him around the world. And some of him would end up in the same place that vacuum cleaners and everything else go sooner or later. The dump.

I turned Granny over to an airline agent.

"Hope Grandpa enjoys the new location." The agent looked around for Grandpa. I patted the cardboard box. "Grandpa," I said.

"Oh, my mother just told me where to scatter her." The agent smiled.

Grandma beamed and asked "Oh really? Where, dear?"

"The casino. She's there every weekend. Loves it. Wants to play the slots for all eternity."

"Oh, how wonderful," Grandma replied.

I left them chatting happily. People skills. Some got it, some don't. Taxi drivers had to or they would go crazy. And broke. No people skills, no tips. No tips, no shoes. I grinned at the $125 that Granny had slipped me. Twenty-five-dollar tip. Those hot red shoes were getting closer to my feet. Maybe my rent would be on time, too.

I trotted back to my ride and hot-pedaled up the turnpike to get back to Belle. I wanted some answers to at least a million questions.

When I pulled up in front of Susan Young's office, I recognized the unmarked cop car parked at the curb. There were lots of possibilities. Susan had discharged a weapon in a courtroom. She had wounded someone, even if it was her asshole husband. Belle was a hooker. Belle was married, apparently to another asshole, but a dead asshole. I shouldn't be surprised to see the cops visiting Susan's office, especially with Belle inside. If it was Jon, I knew he would give me a hard time about letting Belle stay with me.

I strode up the sidewalk. At least I tried to stride because I thought it would give me an air of authority. I should have known better than to think Jon would see me as authoritative. He was leaning on the open doorjamb and looked like he had been waiting awhile. Looking good was part of Jon. I had a sudden urge to reach out and run my hand down his chest.

He knew how long a trip to the airport would take, but he didn't know I had taken Granny, and Grandpa, inside and to security. That had added at least 20 minutes.

"Where've you been? And what are you thinking, getting involved in a police investigation? You're a taxi driver, for Christ's sake. I told you to drop her off."

"Hi to you, too, Lieutenant ... Jon Jon, and how did you know I was going to be here?" I knew he hated to be called Jon Jon. I think it made him feel too young or immature or less authoritative or something. I didn't care what, as long as it distracted him. I wanted some answers from Belle or Susan. I knew that Jon would clam up the minute I started asking questions about an open investigation.

So we had a brief staring contest. Nose to nose. Scowl to scowl. Suddenly, he grinned and ran a finger down my cheek. I tried to swat his hand away, but he was faster than me and grabbed my hand and placed it over his heart.

"Wouldn't want you getting injured in the line of duty. And Willie told me where you would be. Remember, you always call in your location." He kept grinning. I felt my heat rising. I started to lean forward, rethought that idea and jerked away from his grasp. I felt suddenly rebellious. Of course, before that very second, I had been considering saying no to Belle. Now I would insist that she stay with me.

"I just offered Belle a place to stay. It's not like I'm interfering or anything. I'm hardly ever home anyway. I mean between my job and my fabulous social life."

Jon frowned. "I don't know what's going on with this thing yet. I don't need a civilian wandering around where I might have to worry. … What social life?"

"I'm flattered you're worried about me. So now that you've rescued the maiden in distress, you want to go beat your chest or something?"

Jon eyed my chest speculatively.

"Don't even think about it." I backed up another step.

"You're not a maiden … are you?" He realized we had an audience. Belle and Susan were watching our little interaction with fascination.

"I don't want any more casualties. Too much paperwork." He stuffed his hands into his pockets.

"So you're telling me that you don't want Belle to stay with me because there might be danger. Where do you want her to stay? And how much danger are we talking here? If we're talking tire slashing or windshield breaking or sheet-metal denting, I just won't take the taxi home with me."

"Jesus." Jon shook his head as if to clear away some fuzz. "I'm talking about you. I don't give a shit about some car! This is a murder investigation. A person got killed."

Belle mumbled something. "What?" Jon turned on her.

She returned his stare. "I just said that I wasn't sure that Horace could be considered a person. And we don't know that whoever did him is looking at anyone else. I just need a place to regroup. I didn't like the man, but I did know him intimately, and staying where we lived together is just creepy. Okay? Besides, you probably still have all that yellow tape stuff strung around like Christmas lights. You think I want to live with that stuff? It'll kill business." Belle paused, remembering Jon was a cop. She was using her high-class accent but still managed to convey a lot of defiance. "And there must be more evidence you can find," she finished.

"Okay, I get that you can't go back yet. Maybe we could set up some sort of surveillance." Jon turned to me. "I can reroute a squad car by Honey's apartment every hour or so."

He turned back to Belle. "But your 'business' is over now anyway. Nothing happens out of Honey's apartment."

We went back and forth for 15 more minutes. Jon was not happy about Susan or Belle. Susan had just given the legal system the finger when she shot her husband in the lower right cheek in the middle of the most secure place in that system. He still couldn't figure out why she was walking around free, let alone practicing law. I've always felt that lawyers have a way of working the system that the rest of us pay them dearly for. When it involves their own behavior, they can slip through like eels. Susan stayed surprisingly silent, but she had made bail and walked, and that had to irk the hell out of Jon the cop.

Belle baited Jon for a while about her profession and wondered aloud how she would make a living now. He gritted his teeth and didn't say much. We finally settled on me not taking the taxi home and Belle and Susan not telling anyone about the sleeping arrangement. Jon would check in on us in the evening when he could. I figured he would also send a squad car around with or without our approval. This arrangement was going to try my already-limited social capabilities, and I really, really hoped it wouldn't last long.

In the meantime, I had a job. Mona called me.

"You got a pickup at the train station. You remember to pack your mace this morning? I still don't know why you won't get a gun."

"So I won't shoot myself?" I had reluctantly put the mace canister in my oversize bag that morning, hoping I wouldn't spray my face. Weapons are an "oops" kind of situation for me. I headed south on the interstate.

Chapter 3

The train station is in Springfield. Springfield has a history of politicians who have somehow managed to avoid indictment. Their style of leadership seems to have induced a lack of confidence from the general population. Violence is not unheard of. Thus the mace in my bag. The Springfield cabbies might be the toughest in the state. And there are places that even they don't go in that town, no matter what they're packing. A cabbie had been shot recently in Springfield, so everyone was a little on edge.

Once upon a time, the train station was one of those fabulous Grand Central-like structures. They took out the Grand and the Central. Now it looks more like the servants entrance to the castle. It's a wall of spectacular oversize stone blocks, with a door that looks like the neighborhood Laundromat. We just call it "the station."

It's not in a great neighborhood, but the city has a lot of cops on patrol in that area. And hanging flower baskets.

And extra lighting. If they didn't, Amtrak might whip right on through and forget them. Politicians would have to leap from a moving train. To avoid this embarrassing possibility, they keep it safe enough for most passengers to make it from the train to a waiting taxi. Passengers do not linger. Taxis, however, have no choice.

I pulled up to the station in time for the 11 o'clock arrivals. Of course, the train was late. There were three other taxis waiting. Two locals and one from Holyoke. Don't even ask about the crime rate in that city.

The other drivers were out of their cars, smoking or leaning against fenders. Cool Rides drivers aren't allowed to smoke around the car, or eat or drink or have sex or do anything except be nice to customers and drive. I decided to stay in my cab.

I was watching two cabbies in front of me when a parking-enforcement officer pulled up in her gas-powered three-wheeler. She parked on the sidewalk, hopped out and rushed into the building. Based on her posture, my guess was bathroom break. One cabby grunted and chomped down harder on his soggy, smoking, smelly cigar.

The train arriving put every cabby on high alert. The sound of an incoming train triggers a Pavlovian reaction in cabbies. It means money and money means food and rent and clothes and a life.

The first passenger came out of the station lugging a huge suitcase. The second cabby in line opened his back door and trunk. The passenger steered her overstuffed baggage toward him.

The first cab in line was a Springfield Cab, and the driver looked like he was moonlighting from a local semipro hockey team. He was huge and tough and he viewed this fare as his. Unless you've been called ahead, there is a protocol for fetching fares. First cab in line gets first guy off train. And the big guy wanted that fare.

I sunk below window level so as not to get involved. My hand inched over toward my bag and the mace. Thoughts of guns danced in my head.

The drivers were in each other's faces with lots of hand waving and interesting language. The Springfield driver had a gun and was holding it in the air, not pointing at anything special. The other driver had his hand on the one tucked in his pants.

The passenger loaded her luggage in the second cab and slammed the trunk. The sound set off a fight-or-flight reaction in the drivers. Another gun came out, and one of them started firing off rounds. I felt one bullet hit the passenger side of my car. The second two shots connected with the parking cart, which started spurting gas from its now-ruptured tank. One last round was fired off and the second driver dived over the hood of his cab, threw his gun onto the seat and took off, triumphantly, with the fare. Not to be left behind, the local tossed his cigar over his shoulder and pursued. The last I saw of them, they'd run a red light and were flying down the road playing bumper car.

I once saw a program on the Discovery Channel where someone set out to prove that, contrary to urban myth, a gas tank ruptured by a bullet would not explode. They couldn't get theirs to explode, but then again, they didn't have a lighted cigar.

I slunk out to view the damage to my cab.

I was leaning over the hole when my fare appeared.

"Whatcha' doin'?"

I looked up at a young man wearing a black T-shirt that said "my bad ass misses your bad ass" in white letters. I wondered what his parents thought of his college career. Whipping a tissue out of my pocket, I pretended to polish the front fender, strategically placing myself between my passenger and the telltale mark.

"Oh, just taking off a spot of mud." I opened the door for him.

"Thanks." He slid in.

I got in the driver's side and fastened my seat belt. As I pulled out, there was a loud kawhamp. The parking-enforcement cart rose gracefully in the air, sparks erupting from the gas tank. It flipped onto its side, wheels spinning madly, looking like a cockroach that someone hadn't completely squashed. I guess the cigar wasn't as soggy as it looked.

"Holy shit!" My passenger craned his neck to see the smoking ruin.

I nailed the accelerator, heading back to the throughway. The meter maid ran out of the building waving madly. I sped up.

About five miles up the interstate, we passed a taxi on the side of the road. It had a flat tire and two windows with what might have been bullet holes in them and no driver. I ducked and sped up. When you see a burned-out vehicle on the highway in New York City, it's probably an illegal cab with a stolen fare. Cabbies can be really sensitive when it comes to fares.

Once past the larger cities, the scenery turns into pastoral farmland, green forest interspersed with corn and squash. It's like entering a different country when you head north. By the time you get to Northampton, the insanity and violence of the bigger cities seem invisible. That doesn't mean it doesn't exist. It's just more difficult to see. I suspected Lieutenant Jon Stevens saw it all too often. Taxi drivers pick up a pretty good cross section of the population, so I probably had seen the players from the more violent culture to the south. They aren't always obvious, and that was okay with me. If I was driving someone to a drug deal or an assassination, I didn't want to know.

I dropped off my passenger at the college and headed down the hill into town.

I was driving down Main Street when I spotted Jon. I pulled over and stopped. As he strolled over, his eyes were riveted on the passenger-side fender.

"What's that?" he asked. He knelt and traced a finger over the hole. "Looks like a bullet hole."

"What?" I smiled innocently.

"You've been in Springfield again, huh?"

"Train station."

"Drug deal?" He raised an eyebrow in question.

"Cabbie wars."

"Ah. Those cabbies can be temperamental."

"Need a ride? No charge." I leaned over and pushed the door open.

"Is this a bribe?" He got in anyway. "I need to talk to you."

"Uh-oh." I had almost forgotten he was a cop.

"Springfield called." He fiddled with the radio dial. "They seem to think there was a Cool Rides cab at the scene of damage to a city vehicle."

I smiled sweetly at him. "We have five cabs." One of the good things about our cabs is that they are very recognizable. Sometimes that's also a bad thing.

"A woman was driving." He tapped his fingers on the dash and stared into my eyes. "How many women drive for Cool Rides?"

I sighed. "Just me."

"They also were curious whether a Cool Rides driver might know anything about a taxi deserted on the highway. Tires shot out, two windows. You're a scary person."

"What? Hey, I just drive."

"And I'm sure you do a fine job of that. It's the extracurricular stuff that worries me."

"Well then, fasten your seat belt, stud muffin. I'll get you back to the cop house," I said and grumbled. Jon looked at me. A smile played across his mouth.

I pulled away from the curb and was at the police station in about three minutes. Jon stepped out and knelt next to the open window. He glanced at the bullet hole again.

"Don't get that fixed. It may be evidence." His eyes darkened. "Stud muffin? I like that."

"Like my boss can let it alone." I breathed out. "I haven't told him about it yet."

"The stud muffin?"

"The bullet hole, duh."

Jon tapped the door. "I work until 8 tonight. Stop by and give me a statement … please." He said the last word with reluctance, so I nodded in agreement. He sauntered into the cop house, and I enjoyed the view of his backside. Umm. Resistance to whatever I was resisting might be fading.

I swung the cab back around to the Cool Rides office. Since we had agreed that I would stop by and talk about the Springfield shooting incident, that would take care of his evening checkup on Belle and me. There was some heat growing between me and Jon. I wasn't sure I wanted him around my apartment, even with Belle as a chaperone. She was, after all, of a special sexual persuasion. Mostly that it was all right anywhere, any time. And probably better if money changed hands.

I ran two more short hauls. One was an older lady who needed batteries for her flashlights. It took her a half an hour in Radio Shack to match batteries to flashlights. When she was done, the clerk looked like he'd been staring into a thousand-watt bulb. It was an eight-dollar fare and a ten-dollar wait fee. She gave me $25. Sometimes, life is good. I could feel those shoes on my feet. The ones with the sequined heels that I had seen in one of the uptown stores. Where do people wear these shoes? Who cares? I just wanted them to be on my feet, or in my closet.

After I dropped off the flashlight lady, Moanin' called me with a couple of old geezers who had been out shopping for gifts for their girlfriends who shared a birthday. How sweet was that, I thought, noting the address. Oops, the local hard core porn shop. They started pulling crotchless panties, silk handcuffs, and dildos that belonged on an elephant out of the shopping bag, along with some hard-core videos.

"What ya think, lady? You being a woman and all. Should we start with Debbie Does Dallas, or Deep Throat? What would get you most riled up? At our age, we only get one shot at this."

The other one smirked. "Unless we get one of them four-hour erections. Did we get any of that Viagra stuff?"

"Naw, they don't sell that in this store. I think we gotta go to the grocery store."

I wasn't going to redirect their search for Viagra. They had to be 80 years old. The Bobbsey Twins in their golden years. Or, possibly, Tweedledum and Tweedledee. I should have known that having me pick them up in front of the supermarket on the next block was a ruse.

"Deep Throat. If you miss the ending, you can discuss the political implications of the title." I pulled over fast and left them at the retirement complex. When had 80 become the new 30? I was approaching that milestone and I didn't want to think about any age after that.

I dropped the cab off at the office and reluctantly headed over to the cop house on foot. It was 6 o'clock and I was tired and hungry. I had given Belle a key to my apartment and I wanted to get there before she got too comfortable. I had agreed to let her sleep on my couch, but I wanted to be sure she was the only one sleeping, or doing anything else, there.

I stopped at the front desk and picked up the phone to communicate with the cop behind the bullet-proof glass. He looked like a big blue fish stuck in a small glass bowl.

He buzzed me in and I wound my way around the desks and cubicles to find Jon's office. He rose when I paused at the door and motioned me to a chair in the corner. He came around and sat on his desk facing me. That was a good sign. He wasn't trying to intimidate me. I squirmed anyway and he grinned. I shifted my butt deeper into the chair and looked at my feet. When I looked up, his grin had widened. The fact that it made him more attractive pissed me off. I hated my automatic reaction to authority. It was an odd mix of intimidation, defiance and a little respect. Jon wore his authority easily.

"Captain Donnelly called from the Springfield police. It seems that you may have witnessed, or been involved in, the destruction of city property. Namely a parking-enforcement vehicle. It exploded and had to be towed away. Would you know anything about this? And, Honey, let me remind you that I am a cop. Don't even think about lying. Or omitting anything pertinent. I have a lot on my watch right now and I need the cooperation."

"Hey, all I was doing was picking up a fare. I brought him back here. The cabbies down there are crazy. I don't know how they survive. Most of their fares would be just as happy to shoot them." The piece I didn't mention was that one of my recent fares had shot the front seat of my cab before I even went to the train station. But it was an accident. My rule of thumb is to tell the cops as little as possible, and it really wasn't relevant right now anyway.

"Down there they shoot to kill," I said. "I might have to start packing a weapon."

"Oh God, please prevent that." Jon groaned. "You don't need a weapon to cause mayhem. Just tell me what happened."

I related the story of the two cabs playing bumper car and the lighted cigar-gasoline-bullet hole combination. Jon shook his head. I had been running into some pretty bizarre situations recently, but none of it was my fault. This logic is what sane people call denial. I was an accident waiting for a catalyst.

"Okay, I'll call Springfield and clear that up. I don't suppose you got a cab number, license plate or any kind of ID on the two cabs?"

"Uh, no. One was local and the other was from Holyoke. I just kept my head down. And one of those bullets hit my car, too. If you find them, I want to sue their asses." Jon had already seen that bullet mark on my car.

"If anyone finds them, and it won't be me, they won't have two bricks to rub together. Their sorry asses will be behind bars."

Jon stood up and I followed. "So can I go now? I really need to get home and get something to eat." And check up on Belle.

"Come on, I'll give you a ride. We can pick up a pizza on the way. I want to talk to Belle about her future plans, arrange an interview. See what she might know about Horace and what activities might have contributed to his having a hole the size of a baseball in his head."

I wanted to know Belle's plans, too. I sincerely hoped they didn't include turning tricks out of my apartment. I wondered what other job skills she had.

When Jon and I got to the apartment, pizza in hand, Belle was there and had made herself at home. Which was nice because, apparently, being at home included cooking, grocery shopping, and cleaning. My tiny place was spotless, and the fridge was stocked with soda, orange juice, eggs, cheese, and salad makings.

"Oh goody, pizza. I'll make a salad to go with it." She jumped up and headed into the kitchen. I worked to close my mouth. Jon smiled. Maybe a roomie wasn't such a bad idea after all.

When we had settled into the pizza, Jon started the conversation in typical cop fashion.

"So how are you planning to make a living, Belle? Now that Horace is gone. And when can you come into the station for an interview?"

Belle swallowed hard. I was pretty sure she had been telling the truth about not liking Horace, but he must have been a major part of her life, and the fact that someone close to her had been shot dead had to make rational planning difficult. Her temporary solution was that she was living with me. How rational was that? For either of us.

"I don't know what I'm going to do. Maybe I'll go back to school. Smith has a special program for older students. I could add some real diversity to their classes. Bring in some reality checks."

"Yeah," Jon said. "I'm not sure they're going to welcome a former prostitute into classes with impressionable young ladies from rich families. Rich, full-tuition-paying families. It is former, isn't it?" Jon raised an eyebrow at her.

"Oh yeah, I've learned that ho'ing ain't no life. I got better things to do. Maybe I can work part time and do school the rest."

Jon just nodded. They arranged a time to meet the next day.

Chapter 4

The next morning, I headed to the taxi garage and Belle went to face Jon and the cop station. I hadn't learned much more about her. No girl talk. No revelations about Horace or life in the trade. That was okay with me. I hadn't decided just how close I wanted to get to Belle and her problems. They could be pretty overwhelming. She could be overwhelming even without any problems. I might be willing to get some shoe advice from her. And how did she keep those nails so long and perfect? And what did a prostitute do with 2-inch nails? She had some skills I might lack. Not my job skills, but there were lots of other areas of expertise I was willing to learn about. I could see some crossover potential from her former job to my … whatever.

The only time Cool Rides had ever picked up Belle was when I transported her from the courthouse. I had seen her riding in the other company's cabs. Mostly heading south on the interstate. I hadn't asked why she never called us.

When I got to the garage, the parking lot was filled with a bizarre collection of cars and people. I skirted the crowd and went around to the back door.

"What's with the misfits?" I asked Mona.

"We have five cars and three drivers. I ran an ad for new drivers."

She held up a stack of applications.

"We have interviews every 15 minutes starting right now. Since you're officially management, you get to help."

We looked out the window at the line of people scrambling to establish a pecking order.

A guy with arms bulging out of a black T-shirt that declared "FUCK you" to the world made it almost to the front of the line and shoved a small blond person of indeterminable gender backward into the bosom of a well-endowed woman, where it was swallowed by oversize breasts.

An old lady stood at the head of the line brandishing a heavy cane. Even Mr. FUCK you wasn't getting by her.

She backed in the door, waving her cane, and hobbled to the visitor's chair. Folding her hands in her lap, she stared blankly at the wall.

"You must be Margaret Snazhour." Mona looked up.

At the sound of a voice, Margaret Snazhour refocused her gaze.

"I'm here to be a taxi driver. What do I have to do to become one?"

"You need a valid driver's license. And you can't have any felonies on your record." Mona paused. Margaret Snazhour stared in Mona's direction.

"Do you have any felonies on your record?" I asked.

Margaret smiled serenely. "Not yet." She moved her eyes in my direction. "Do you think I need one?" She glanced around to see if a new felony might pop up and help her fit in …or get the job.

"We'll call you." Mona helped Margaret to the door and yelled "Edwardo Szezmecki, you're up next."

Mr. FUCK you sauntered in.

"Do you have a dress code? 'Cause I don't need nobody telling me how to dress. I need to let the assholes I pick up know who they're dealing with. I want 'em to see these." He flexed his arm muscles impressively. He watched his biceps wiggle for a few seconds.

"I gotta be able to tell 'em to fuck off if I need to. What kind of weapons do we carry? Does the company supply me with a gun? Or do I gotta bring my own?"

"We'll call you," said Mona and yelled out the next name.

Stewart Slipslit, the blond, gender-ambiguous person, came next.

"Do you have any driving experience?" Mona asked.

"I've always wanted to drive. I just worship Dale Earnhardt Jr. I bet I could make those cars do things you never dreamed of. I bet I could make Jr. do things he's never dreamed of." He smiled. "And I've only been busted once. It's still pending. I would never have solicited such a brute. God! He was sooo ugly. I'm going to fight this charge like horse cocky. Does the company provide legal counsel?"

Another application hit the round file.

"You get the next one." Mona handed me the clipboard and fled to the bathroom.

"Bobby DeBenny, come on down," I yelled over the crowd. A man and a woman fought to get through the door. It was the Keystone Cops making a big entrance through a small door.

"Which one of you is Bobby DeBenny?"

"I am," replied the woman.

"I was born first." The guy shoved her backward and slammed the door behind him.

"We're twins. But I'm better for this job."

"Robert – that's me – and Roberta. That's her." He waved a dismissive hand in the direction of the parking lot.

We ended the interviews two hours later with only one application not in the wastebasket.

We had gone through a guy who wanted to know if our insurance covered him if he accidentally ran over his neighbor and killed him. "Who, by the way, is boffing my wife," he said and asked if the company provided personal-injury lawyers free of charge to its drivers. Mona pushed him out the door.

She almost beheaded a large, muscular man who asked if he had to take orders from a fat old lady like her or did we have a real man in charge somewhere.

When the last applicant had come in, he seemed sort of close to almost normal.

"Got any driving experience?" Mona inquired.

"God is my guide. I trust he will steer for me. Can I offer you some literature?"

We really needed drivers.

The rest of my day was made up of short-haul fares, which meant a lot of driving and not a lot of income. Fortunately, I got a couple of good tips.

I picked up a British woman at the in-town hotel, where shopping, coffee, entertainment, drug dealers and casual prostitutes are all within an easy walk. There are at least two coffee shops on each block to reboot energy levels continuously. Good shopping, good food and good everything else.

She wanted to go to the mega-mall outside Holyoke. I sighed. We motored off to the acres of concrete.

Like malls around the country, this one has killed the inner city as a shopping district. That's why cabbies going into downtown Holyoke carry at least a can of mace. But the mall is an easy run off the interstate, and the likelihood of car, or driver, returning with bullet holes is slim.

I picked her up two hours later. She smiled a well-sated-woman smile and handed me a really big tip.

I smiled about paid-up rent, dropped the queen of the mall off at the hotel and called the office.

The next fare was the Smoker. Mostly, we run errands for him. Today he wanted a ride downtown.

His living space reflected his belief that it is dangerous to be more than six inches from some form of nicotine. Cigarettes were stacked against the wall in cartons, boxes, and individual packs. Loose singles were lying around on every available surface. Plan ahead for the apocalypse in case it didn't include smokes. Lately, he had started adding nicotine patches to his stash. This was not an effort to cut back on his smoking. He had two patches on his arm and a lighted cigarette hanging from his lips.

I staggered back from the intensity of the secondhand smoke, held my breath and bolted outside to suck clean air.

I stashed his walker in back and checked his seat belt. When he died, it wouldn't be from putting his head through my windshield. After dropping him in town, I rolled down windows and turned the air conditioner on high. Sometimes I did a two-exit run down the interstate to deodorize the cab afterward. But he tipped really well.

The last fare was a trip to the convenience store. One of our regulars needed toilet paper. Mona suggested I shop and deliver. It would save me airing out the cab again and save them $9. I zipped from the corner fast mart to the apartment.

"Ah do appreciate this. We was usin' coffee filters 'cause we run out of everything else. Kinda rough on the rear, if ya know what ah mean."

I snatched the 10-dollar bill and scurried to the cab.

When I dragged myself home, Belle was in the kitchen cooking. Jon was leaning back in a chair, flipping through television channels. I liked the cooking thing. I looked at Jon. A roomie might cramp my style there.

Jon had had a formal interview with Belle in a formal interview room with a recorder running. Which had accomplished nothing.

Right now, I could tell he was rolling something around in his brain and no amount of ass wiggling from me was going to bring him back to this planet.

I was curious why Belle never used Cool Rides unless the police made the phone call, so I switched my focus to her. No other cab company in town had cars as nice as ours. And their drivers … ugh.

Belle served dinner on the kitchen table, which was actually in my living room, which would also be the guest bedroom.

"So Belle," I said, "why don't you use Cool Rides when you go to Springfield or Holyoke?"

Jon's attention shifted to Belle. He watched her like a retriever eyeing a tennis ball.

"Horace always made the arrangements." She looked at me, away from Jon's cop face. "I figured he had an agreement." She knew that Jon didn't care about her profession unless it related to the unnatural death Horace had experienced.

"Horace usually came with me. He said he wanted to check out the clientele, make sure they wouldn't give me any grief. But he never came inside. They could have been space aliens for all he knew. And, Honey, those other drivers? They're huge. I never had one that didn't scare me just to look at him. I always thought they were packin', too. They sat like they had a lump up their butts. I would have used Cool Rides but Horace said your boss wasn't accommodating enough."

"Yeah, since the shootout at the train station, he's been taking all the Springfield and Holyoke calls himself or letting Andrew do it. We really need to get some new drivers." I rested my head on my hand. I was ready for bed.

"I thought you had enough drivers." Jon looked at me.

"What about that big guy? He would have been good for those runs, maybe even for late-night bar runs."

"Willie won't do bar runs. Doesn't want barf in the car. And the big guy got a less stressful job as a jail guard. We're down to two drivers plus Willie."

Belle looked at me speculatively. "So, what's it pay?"

I stared at her, thinking about the day of interviews we'd had. Well, she beat any of them. As long as she wasn't using the car for her own business ventures, Willie might not hold her previous job experience against her. She would be good company when business was slow, she had lots of people experience, taxi driving was a service job – and she'd been in a service profession. Sort of.

"I've been thinking about a career change. I need to lower my stress level. Men have expectations when they're paying. Besides, I'm tired of having strange things in my mouth."

I swallowed hard.

"How often you been busted?" Jon knew the rules for driving a cab in Northampton.

"Me?" Belle shook her head indignantly. "Never. No, uh-uh, not ever. Not even a parking ticket. I'm smarter than the law."

Jon knew better than to start a pissing contest with Belle. "I mean that you can't have a record if you want to get a taxi-driving license. The first thing they do is run your vitals through the police database."

"Then what was the tracking bracelet for?" I asked.

"I was a witness. And we won't go there. Suffice it to say I will pass the felony check with flying colors." Belle adopted her British accent. I was beginning to enjoy the way she played with her language skills.

"Tell me more about Horace and the other cab companies." Jon wanted to pull on that string for a while.

I wanted to know more about the tracking bracelet, but Belle had decided to stop talking. The conversation continued, mostly from Jon's side. He kept trying to get information from Belle, who clearly wasn't ready to implicate herself or anybody, living or dead, in illegal activity. She smiled her best "kiss my butt, copper" smile and kept silent.

He finally stood up. "I'm going home. Long day tomorrow, researching local taxi companies." He gave Belle a look.

"Could I see you outside?" He turned to me.

"Yeah, sure." Whatever he wanted, spying on Belle wasn't on my agenda. I stepped into the hall and shut the door.

Jon grabbed the back of my neck and pulled me up to his face. I was too startled to resist, or didn't want to, when he planted his lips on mine. It was one of those romance-novel kisses. Started out gentle and ended with my toes curled in knots, my arms around his neck and my body plastered against him. Wow. It had been way too long since I felt like this. His hands sort of wandered down toward my rear end. Then they came back up and circled my waist. I liked them down lower. He pulled back and smiled slowly. I looked encouraging.

"Honey, you just might have opened this case up for me." He ran his finger down my cheek and his thumb over my lips. Now I was awake. His eyes were dark and unreadable. Of course, the hallway was also dark and unreadable.

"Thanks." He kissed me softly on the forehead and was off down the stairs. What kind of goodnight is that? What did he do when he wanted to stay? If that was just a "thank you, dear," what was his seduction arsenal? I staggered a little and went back inside to Belle.

Belle eyed me with the disdain of experience.

"Man, that is one hot behind. Too bad he's a cop. And get rid of the shit-eating grin."

"Wait a minute. What's wrong with being a cop?"

"Honey, what's not wrong with being a cop?"

"Hey, he's a good guy." I didn't have all that much invested in Jon, but I could see potential and I didn't want my temporary roomie dissing him. "He could say the same kind of stuff about you and your profession."

"My profession is the oldest in the world," Belle said. "Besides, I'm thinking about changing it. Self-employment sucks. Horace considered me an independent contractor so he didn't give bennies, and who can afford health insurance these days?"

She wanted out of the Jon discussion, clearly. I wasn't sure how I felt about Jon the cop myself, but my reasons were different from hers. The pull was getting stronger. My libido had kicked up a notch, and my curiosity about what could happen was rising faster than a teenage boy's hard-on. Jon and I would have some major control issues.

Like who would be in charge of my life. When he had arrested me, in another lifetime, it was clear that he had standards of behavior I might not share.

"So tell me more about this taxi-driving thing." Belle finished the dishes.

"Come down in the morning and meet Willie and Mona. If you're still serious, Willie will give you a driving test. See if you're any good." I knew Willie's driving tests. You needed near-worshipful reverence for the car. No on and off the gas, no sudden braking, no tailgating, no speeding. Well, no getting caught. Willie was a speeder most of the time. Especially airport runs. But he never did it with a passenger in the car, and he never got caught. He had a sixth sense about radar traps.

Besides, after Belle figured out the change in pay scale from her previous employment, I didn't think she would be interested in taxi driving no matter what the bennies were.

"I'm hitting the sack." I tossed some sheets and a pillow to her.

"Enjoy the couch." It may have been shorter than Belle.

"Hey, I done worse." She pulled it out into a bed and spread the sheets.

Chapter 5

I opened my eyes to daylight and coffee. Coffee? Oh yeah, Belle. I mumbled something about dumb-ass whores that I hoped I never said in public and staggered into the kitchen/living/dining/guest bedroom. I resented sharing my space until I saw the kitchen table. Apparently, my mother and Belle shared the belief that breakfast is the most important meal of the day. I grabbed a toasted sesame bagel and smeared it with garden-crunchy cream cheese. I couldn't remember the last time I had used my toaster. I was surprised it worked. How about that? I had a working toaster. How domestic. The fresh-ground coffee was a mystery. I was pretty sure I didn't have a coffee grinder in my itsy, bitsy kitchen. Even the coffee pot was a surprise.

"Jeez, what do I owe you for all this food?"

"Consider it rent." Belle poured coffee into one of the free ceramic mugs from the Cool Rides closet of promotional junk. Advertising companies sent samples of stuff we could use to get people to ride with Cool Rides, sometimes spelled Cool Rode, sometimes Cool Ribs. We didn't need more customers. We needed more drivers for the customers we had.

"I need to go to the office with you today, Mom. Take-your-girl-to-work day. Remember that idea? Wonder what they'd think of me taking a kid to work. Anyway, I need to impress your boss with my skills and abilities." She didn't specify which skills and abilities.

"You'll have to impress Mona first. Then you'll need to get Willie to let you near a car. He's very protective. Then you go to City Hall and apply for a taxi-driving license," I mumbled around my last bite of bagel. "Yeah, I'll take you in. They need people right now, and I actually think you might make a pretty good driver."

She would fit the Cool Rides driver profile. Because we didn't have a driver profile. People tried it and we waited to see if they stuck around. If they didn't get freaked out by the insanity of the population they served, they might stay. We went through a lot of drivers.

She raised an eyebrow. "Why, thanks. I think."

When we were tanked on coffee, we headed, on foot, to the office. I was in my usual driving uniform of black jeans, T-shirt and sneakers. Belle was in her own professional outfit of spandex black pants, gold glitter top and 4-inch spiked red heels.

Northampton is a city of believers. We buy into all the major religions and most of the minor ones. Even nonbelieving is a belief system in Northampton. People here pay attention to their convictions.

As we passed one of the many churches in town, the sound of singing drifted out the open windows. Belle stopped. She stared at the church. It was one of those New England Postcard Moments. White spire reaching into clear blue sky, the sound of music coming out of the arched windows. And Belle, in her special spandex and really special shoes, heading up the sidewalk toward the church. That would add a Northampton moment.

"It's nice to listen," I called after her, "but we should probably get to the office."

"We gotta go in." Belle stared at the open door.

"Well, I guess …" I followed her up the steps. It was choir practice, so the pews were empty, but I knew they were okay with an audience. I'd stopped in to listen before. I squeezed by Belle and paused at the back, ready for a quick escape. When the music stops, so does my belief in the almighty.

I sat down in the last row of seats. Belle ignored me and walked to the front. The choir began a song and stumbled on the first few bars. Belle, in her glittered glory, might have distracted them.

At the first pause in the singing, Belle suddenly rose. "No, no, no. That part needs a solo And it needs some love. That guy is asking God to save his soul, so you better put yours into it. Like this."

And she began to sing. Her voice pulled the heart right out of the song. The minister's mouth dropped open and his eyes bugged out. The choir stared until Belle raised her arms and said, "Now you come in and give me some support here."

She brought her arms down with a flourish and they followed her. At the end of the stanza, she lowered her voice into a hum and ended with "amen."

"Well, won't you join us?" The minister was ready to adopt Belle no matter what her fashion statement.

"Oh, I gotta run right now. Job interview. But I could come back if you have another rehearsal later."

The reverend grabbed a schedule off the table and thrust it at her.

"I didn't know you were religious," I said as Belle clattered down the walkway.

"Oh, I ain't religious. I just like good music. Gospel is good music. My momma took me to church. I sang in the choir until I was 16 and found other outlets."

I wanted to ask more about Belle's other outlets, but we had arrived at Cool Rides.

Mona was standing out front, overflowing her tank top and tapping her toe. Our visit to church had made us 15 minutes late. My shift started at 9 every morning, Monday through Friday, sometimes Saturday and Sunday. Maybe having a new driver possibility in tow would make up for the 15 minutes.

"You got a Holyoke pickup in 10." Mona never wasted time when a fare was involved.

"Good morning to you, too. This is Belle. She's interested in driving for us." I gave Belle a little goose to push her into Mona's sphere of focus.

"Unnh!" Belle gave me a dirty look. "Pleased to meet you, I'm sure." She used her most queenly accent.

Mona looked her over carefully. "Don't I know you from somewhere?"

Uh-oh. Mona kept pretty careful tabs on the competition. She might have seen Belle in the other company's cars. It wasn't my business to bring up applicants' previous professions. Mona's attitude about sex for hire might be different from mine. She would not tolerate it coming back on the company. Or spilling over into the backseat.

"You ever done any professional driving?" Mona's eyes moved over Belle's eye-popping outfit. I thought about Mr. FUCK you. We needed drivers and we needed them fast. It was more about attitude than fashion anyway.

"I have been in a car in a professional capacity."

"Well, someone has to pick up this guy in Holyoke. Gimme your diver's license and I'll run it up to City Hall. You gonna save me some time and let me know if you got any problems that might show up on the police records, right?"

"Ma'am, I ain't ever been in that kind of trouble." Belle had reverted to her street talk as she handed over her license. Mona gave her an odd look. "And I know Holyoke like the back of my beautiful butt. I can get you anywhere in that uuugly city."

"You can't drive the cab until you have the taxi license." Mona glanced at the Massachusetts driver's license. "Jacobsen? Where's that come from?"

"South African. My mother was a cleaning lady from Jo'burg. My father was an American diplomat. Boy, did they have nothing in common. Produced me, and there ain't nothing common there."

"You can navigate while I drive. I'll split the tip with you if you get me where we need to be," I said. I didn't know interior Holyoke, because Willie never let me drive there. He thought it was too dangerous for a woman. I thought it was too dangerous for anyone. I use the GPS when I need to, but it can't read socioeconomic deprivation from outer space.

"Where's Willie?" I looked at Mona.

"He went to the train station. After your last pickup there, he decided not to let you draw any more fire."

"Nice of him to care."

"Not you. The car. He found the bullet hole."

"Oh, yeah." I hadn't mentioned the shot that connected with the car. "He hasn't fixed it, has he?" I remembered Jon had asked me not to touch it. A bullet was still embedded in the passenger seat. No need to say anything about that one either.

Mona sighed. "No, he figured why bother? You'd just add something new if he went to the trouble. Andrew is on his way to the airport. You're all I got. So get going." She handed me the slip with pickup address, drop-off and cellphone number. No name.

We headed to the car. I slid behind the wheel. Belle jammed herself into the passenger seat. The car was going to handle differently with her riding shotgun. I showed her how to enter the pickup address into the GPS and off we went.

"The GPS is going to tell me the fastest route, but it won't know shortcuts. And it won't tell me where the high-crime areas are, so if you know a better way, tell me."

Shortcuts are important. The more fares you cram into a working day, the faster the rent gets paid. And the sooner you get new, sexier undies. My underwear drawer needed help, especially if Jon was ever going to see it.

We were approaching the first Holyoke exit when Belle said, "Go to the next exit. I know a way to get there faster. This is the exit that wussy people use. We gonna do the drug runner's route."

"What?" I yelped. Too late. I was past the exit my GPS had told me to take.

"Please execute a legal U-turn as soon as possible." The soft feminine computer voice pleaded with me. She obviously knew that this shortcut was going to cause nothing but grief. Maybe they did program in social conditions.

"Recalculating route," the voice whispered. It had given up on the U-turn concept.

"Yeah, yeah, see? You got a built-in wuss in this here car. I went this way a couple of times with Horace. Came back this way, too. You just gotta drive right through. Don't stop for nuthin'. Anyone step out in front of the car, just go around. Or through if you gotta. But don't stop."

Yikes. "What about stop signs? Or stoplights?"

"Honey, don't nobody care in this neighborhood. You just slow down enough not to get broadsided by some other fool running the light from the other direction."

"Aaack," I said. "Why don't you just shoot me?"

"Cause I left my gun in Horace's place and I'm not going back there just yet. 'Sides, I wouldn't shoot you. I'd shoot whoever is shooting at you. 'Cause they might hit me by mistake."

"It wouldn't be a mistake. Next time the GPS wins. It knows better."

"Humph." Belle went into a sulk. "I ain't sayin' anymore. You can find your own way to whatzit street."

"Oh no, no, no. You got us into this place. You better get me out of here." I slammed the brakes with both feet as a guy the size of a football field stepped in front of the cab. His pants were drooping and dirty, his shirt was long-sleeved despite the hot summer weather and he was waving a greasy rag at my windshield. I managed to stop a good six inches from his shinbone.

He started to run the rag over the front window. Belle jumped out and screamed, "Get out of our way, mutha-fucka. I'm on a mission here and I don't need no slowing down." She was almost as big as the window washer and a hell of lot more vocal. She shoved her middle finger over the hood and into his face. He slunk back to the curb.

"Huh." She lowered herself back into the car and fastened the seat belt. "Forward, James," she said, adopting her alternate personality.

I had to smile. We didn't have any more dents or bullet holes in the car … yet.

"Thanks, I guess." I looked over at Belle. She looked pleased with herself. Maybe this was a good time to satisfy some of my curiosity.

"What did Horace do when he came down to Holyoke with you?"

She stared at me for 10 seconds, which is a long time when you're on the receiving end of a stare.

She humphed again and turned her head and most of the rest of her body toward the window.

Okay, that seemed to be a dead end. I had lots of other things I was curious about with Belle. Like the language thing.

"So tell me about your speech thing, like the accent."

Belle turned back toward me. This was safe territory for discussion.

"It's like any language. Once you know the basics, different dialects are easy. You just instinctively know when to use what." She paused. "Like right now, I'm talking to you in American English."

She was right. I hadn't even noticed the transition.

"But that guy back there? He needed something more direct, though it would have been interesting if I'd used the more complex cadence of the Queen's English." She finished properly, smiling. I felt like I might have just broken through a communications barrier. I decided to ask about touchy subjects again.

"I don't mean to pry, Belle, but come on. I'm going to be pretty close to you for a while. I'd like to know if the shooters are looking for anyone who knew Horace or what he did when he was in Holyoke. Or if they're targeting you."

"Yeah, well, I don't know what that creep did. I just did my thing, which, as you know, would be done with some privacy. Horace didn't hang around while I was working. I never did threesomes, and nothing kinky."

"Did he get a ride back with you?"

"Sometimes. Sometimes not."

"You think he was doing something on the side that someone didn't like?"

"How the hell would I know? What I know right now is that you should be driving and I'm gonna navigate." She pronounced it naveegate. "And you should be hangin' a left here. Now." She waved abruptly at the upcoming corner.

I screeched around the turn and almost clipped a black Lincoln Town Car parked by the curb. The driver was leaning against the front fender, smoking a cigarette. He jumped out of my way, dropping the butt as he scrambled. He was making a properly pissed-off gesture with his hand when he saw Belle. His expression changed from anger to surprise. I saw all this in milliseconds, but the expression was hard to miss.

"I guess these things don't handle the corners all that well, huh?" Belle looked back over her shoulder and hunched down in the seat.

"Someone you know?" I asked.

The driver got into his car fast and screeched out to follow us.

"Please take a right at the next intersection." The computer voice took me off guard. I did as requested, and the computer said, "You have arrived." I jammed on the brakes.

We were in front of the Holyoke police station. Huh. The Lincoln Town Car barreled by us as we pulled into the visitor's parking space. The passenger-side window rolled down. A large man leaned out. His face was dark, his hair slicked back. Even at 30 miles an hour, the wind didn't put one hair on his head out of place.

He stared at Belle. She pretended not to notice, but she

turned away and tried to get smaller. Not easy. The town car disappeared around a corner.

"This is where we're picking up?" Belle looked at the gray cement building. It was pretty depressing. "Mona didn't say anything about cops." Maybe because Mona didn't know Belle had an allergy to them.

"This is the address on the fare slip. Why don't you go in and tell the desk sergeant that the Cool Rides taxi is here. I'll stay and guard the car." I turned the key and took it out of the ignition. Picking up at a police station isn't unusual for taxi drivers. People making use of the short-stay option in the holding cells have often had their cars towed, confiscated or wrecked. I once spent an hour driving a guy around from the police station to the bank to the registry to the parking clerk and finally to the tow lot. He'd been driving drunk on an expired registration with four overdue parking tickets, and he stuck his fist in the face of the cop who stopped him. Including my fare, the previous evening had cost him $500 in cash. Lots of stops at the ATM. He didn't tip, but I made a good hourly wage.

"Number one," said Belle, "I don't do police stations. Number two, which of us do you think is going to guard anything against anyone better here, you or me?" She drew herself up until her head touched the roof. She had a point, but I had the car keys.

We had reached a stand off when the fare sauntered down the steps of the station house. It was Jon. I shouldn't have been surprised. Due to the drug trade along the interstate corridor, there was a lot of back-and-forth between the Northampton cops and the Holyoke station.

"Hello, ladies." His smile made me grip the steering wheel harder.

Chapter 6

"Belle," Jon greeted her. "New career choice?"

Mona must have told someone in the cop house that Belle was going to be with me. And that someone knew Jon. That someone had radioed him at the Holyoke station, telling him Belle and I were together. Any of the Holyoke or Northampton cruisers could have transported Jon home. Sometimes people trapped in cars together get more talking done than hours of formal intimidation can achieve, and Jon had gotten nada so far from Belle. This was an innovative approach to interrogation.

"Hey, I could drive like a NASCAR guy if you coppers could admit that I don't got any felonies." She was back in her streetwise hooker character.

"The application is being processed as we speak." Jon showed her his smile and almost batted his eyelashes. Few women are immune to Jon when he turns on the charm. "You have a good teacher." The information about Belle's application must have been radioed to him. He turned his smile on me.

"Uugh. I don't need teachin'. I could drive you guys into the ground. Just gimme a car." Apparently, Belle was one of the few.

I eased the car away from the curb.

"Fasten your seat belt, please." I imitated the computer.

"So, has Willie met Belle yet?" Jon asked as he clicked himself in.

"Nope." Belle turned in her seat. "But what's not to love? He gonna turn me loose on all this here people-movin'."

I drove up the ramp onto the interstate toward Northampton and glanced in the mirror to check traffic. What I saw was big, square, and black. Shit! The Lincoln Town Car was right behind me.

"Hey, Belle, check your side mirror. That anybody you know?"

Jon jerked around in his seat to see what I was talking about. Belle had sunk down in the passenger seat and was trying to make herself as invisible as a 6-foot African queen could. Even with the seat belt strangling her, her hair stuck up above the headrest. I would have laughed, but the car behind us seemed too sinister. Whoever was in it had no way of knowing we had a police officer with us. It would be unusual for a Northampton detective to call a cab when he was on company business. It would be more likely that we had an overnighter from the drunk tank and were an easy mark if they had some business with one of us. Like Belle.

"Shit, that's one of Joe Scarpelli's goons." Jon turned around. "Belle, if you got something to tell me, now's the time. Just how bad might these guys want to talk to you?"

"I don't know what they want. Why you pickin' on me? You the cop. Maybe you done something to piss them off. Maybe we should just shove you out the door and see if they stop."

Jon wasn't happy with the answer. I kept driving as fast as my little car could handle. We were on the interstate in two lanes of traffic. Traffic was light, but I really didn't want to go over 90 in a car that weighs, maybe, a couple thousand pounds, while I was playing dodge-'em with one that was at least double that. The Town Car was right on my bumper. There was no way I was going to outrun it. The car was going 90 and my mind was doing warp speed when I saw two 18-wheelers blocking both lanes ahead of us. I had to slow down.

The Lincoln pulled up beside us. The tinted window rolled down slowly. Like someone right out of the Godfather movies, the guy in the passenger seat raised one hand and made a gun shape with his thumb and finger. Then he pretended to pull the trigger. Personally, I thought it was tacky. But Jon took it more seriously. He lowered his window, leaning his hand on the edge. He was holding his badge. It's hard to have an effective conversation with someone in another car at high speeds, but Jon was doing a pretty good job of it. He held the badge up so they couldn't mistake it, and the big black car dropped back out of sight. I saw it pulling off the exit. Another crisis averted. How many more before Belle wanted to talk? And was she the target? And what did she know? I hate not knowing things.

I pulled off at the first Northampton exit. "Where do you want me to drop you?" I asked Jon.

"I'll go to Cool Rides with you." He leaned his head back against the seat, his eyes closed. He had moved from adrenaline-pumping confrontation to comatose in five minutes. Of course, so had I, but I probably didn't do it as often.

"Belle," he said, "if you tell me anything you know, they might decide it's better to ignore you. If they think you're the only loose end, they'll keep coming after you. You're putting yourself in more danger by not talking to me."

Belle leaned her head against the window. We pulled in front of the garage. I parked and we all sat for a minute. Belle turned to Jon.

"I don't know everything Horace was into." She paused and sighed. "But I can make some experienced guesses and give you some leads."

Jon looked at her funny and I realized she had switched back to her kiss-the-queen accent.

"She's bilingual," I said. Maybe her reality was in between. Jon's reality seemed to be 'take whatever comes at you and deal with it.' He got out of the car, opened Belle's door and put out his hand. She took it and rose with that dignity she did so well. Another technique I might study.

"Let's go inside and talk," he said. I followed them, feeling like the odd one out. Given our company, being odd sort of fit in.

Chapter 7

Jon got three chairs from around the office. Apparently he wanted me to join them, and I figured I had a right to know what Belle said. She was living with me and I didn't want to be blindsided by some goon who was looking for her and found me instead.

"I just have suspicions." Belle slumped in the chair. "I won't testify in court. And I don't have any proof, but I might point you in a direction. I guess I owe Horace that much. It just never seemed like he was into anything very dangerous."

"You don't owe Horace," Jon said. "But I'll take whatever you can give me. It might keep some trouble away from you, too."

"Do I get any protection out of this deal?" Belle looked at Jon. I thought about my little apartment. Did I get protection? Did I need it?

After 40 minutes of talk, Jon had learned almost nothing about Horace's death but quite a lot about the transportation of various illegal substances up the interstate. According to Belle, Horace had been in regular contact with some oversize guys she thought worked for both Scarpelli and one of the many taxi companies in the area. This was probably of more interest to a vice cop than to homicide, but it did create some motives for Horace's untimely trip to Neverland. She'd also heard some vague rumblings about discontent in the Scarpelli family.

"Horace talked a lot but didn't say much. About anything. He acted real nervous around the taxi drivers. Who wouldn't be? They were some scary guys."

Belle stretched her arms over her head. Her large, very visible breasts rose. I watched Jon's eyes follow. He looked down at the table and smiled, shaking his head. Maybe Belle's sexuality was natural, but maybe it was a little overdone. And maybe I could take a few lessons from her. So much to learn, so little time.

"I need something to drink. What you got around here that's cold?" Belle glanced at the Coke machine on the far side of the room. "That thing needs quarters, I bet." She rummaged in her bag and came up with two quarters. I stuck my hand and then my head into my own oversize bag. No matter how much I tried to contain it, the loose change always found its way to the bottom. I came up with two more. Jon produced two out of his pocket. How do men cram all the necessities of life into their pockets? Belle collected the quarters and headed off. He did carry a gun, though. And it wasn't in his pocket.

"It's a little temperamental," I said to her swaying backside.

She put in the required six quarters and pressed a button. Nothing happened.

"Open the door," I said.

She gave the door a yank, but the machine had changed its mind and stayed obstinately closed. Belle moved to the side. She gave it a shove and pulled on the door again. She grabbed the machine with both hands and started shaking it.

"It's not nice to mess with Belle, you fucking machine," she said, shoving it harder. I guess her adrenaline was still running high.

"Don't do that!" I yelled. "It reacts badly to violence."

She gave it one last shove. The door sprang open, crashing against the wall. Soda cans cascaded onto the floor, rolling around erratically.

"Cool!" Belle looked satisfied with the havoc. "Want one?"

"I expect every one of those cans to be put back," I heard Mona growl from the inner office. I think she owns a share in Coke. She's very protective of the ancient machine.

Belle leaned over and picked up a can of Diet Coke.

"Don't – I managed to gurgle out before, pointing it away from herself, she pulled the tab open. Jon, who had better reflexes, jumped out of the line of fire. Soda sprayed over the floor, the table and the other soda cans and splattered against my hair, down my clean white T-shirt and onto my jeans.

"– do that." I was head-to-toe sticky.

"Oops," Belle said, giggling. She turned to Mona. "Got any towels?"

"Enough for the floor. Blondie needs a shower."

I looked down at my clothes. Clean this morning, laundry by nightfall. Shit. Another stellar evening at the Laundromat.

"And don't forget you have an airport this afternoon." Mona surveyed the disaster. "I expect that mess cleaned up by anyone who might want a job here in the future." She stared pointedly at Belle.

"Does that mean my application went through?" Belle pumped the air with her fist.

"Never had them process one so quickly before." Mona glanced over at Jon, who was studying the floor. It certainly warranted a good looking over. "Give me a photo and I'll have it laminated. I need 25 bucks to give to City Hall," she said, her attention back on Belle.

Belle started rummaging in her bag again.

"I guess I'll go home and change," I muttered to myself. No one else seemed to be paying any attention to my problems.

"I'll go with you." Ah, except Jon. "It's on my way to the station. Sticky is cute on you." He was looking at my wet T-shirt, about chest level. His eyes darkened a bit. He raised his gaze and grinned.

I narrowed my eyes at him, but I didn't object to his company. I wasn't about to stay and help Belle clean the floor.

Jon opened the door for me. I swung my bag over my shoulder and sashayed out, trying hard to maintain some dignity and maybe add the sexy walk that Belle did so well.

Jon held my arm as we started walking. "I don't like the Scarpellis' involvement in all this. Maybe you should rethink this sleeping arrangement with Belle. She could stay in a motel somewhere."

"You think that finger-gun thing was because of Belle? I, uh, kind of came close to sideswiping their car before I picked you up." I was pretty sure they wouldn't have gone after me if I had been alone. But I really didn't want Jon telling me what I should do.

"You sideswiped them?" Jon grinned. "I don't think they would have followed you for that. It is Holyoke. Either they recognized Belle or something else is going on." We started up the hill toward my apartment. I live a few blocks from work and just around the corner from the police station, the Laundromat and the bakery. In Northampton, everything is just around the corner. My apartment was on the second floor, above the deli.

I stopped to get food to keep my stomach quiet during the airport run. The teenager behind the counter didn't say anything about the stripe of soda down my front. Of course, he had a pierced lip, nose, eyebrow and ears, a tattoo running the length of his arm and a purple and green Mohawk. His fashion statement trumped mine.

Jon grabbed the bags and followed me up the staircase. I knew he was trying to get more information about Belle. I didn't have any, but it's always good to make a man carry groceries.

I reached into my bag for keys. There's a little hook on one end of my oversize, overstuffed bag for keys. Are they ever there? Not in my lifetime.

I looked up to avoid tripping on the last stair and stopped. The door to my apartment was open, swinging in the breeze. The frame was shattered where the lock had been.

Chapter 8

Jon was behind me, but he hadn't had his head in a bag. He slipped in front and drew his gun. He put his hand up to tell me to stay put. Dream on, Jon Jon. I was right behind him.

Then I saw the inside of my living space. Oh God, oh Christ, oh shit! They'd trashed it. Jon was crouched low, gun in front of him. He moved around the open door and slid behind the upended sofa. I peered around the broken doorjamb. He rose and was in the bedroom in one stride. Long strides, small space. It took about 30 seconds to be certain that no one was inside. My dishes were broken and scattered on top of a mound of what food had been in the fridge. A pair of my sexiest silk panties were hung like a pot holder over the stove. They had ketchup dripping down the front.

"Honey, I told you to stay outside." Jon paused, surveying the damage. "I'm really sorry. Looks like you and Belle need new living arrangements."

I had saved every penny I made for a year to get this place. I spent six months on Willie's couch at the office of the cab company and lived in subsidized housing for six months after that. Whoever "they" were, they had no right. It was broad daylight next to one of the busiest stores in town. Somebody must have seen them. Part of me wanted revenge. The rest of me wanted to hide somewhere safe. Shit!

Jon had his cell phone out.

"Who are you calling?" I was pacing around, working off some of my outrage.

"I'm getting some crime-scene guys over here." He held the phone to his ear with one hand and reached out with his other arm and pulled me against him. I wanted to cry. I wanted to curse. I just laid my head on his chest and closed my eyes.

"Tonight, you can stay at my place. We can't clean up until the crime scene is processed anyway. You don't want to stay in this stuff. And you really do need a shower." Jon dropped the phone into his pocket. I backed up a step.

"I have a job. I have an afternoon airport run. I promised Mona. I've got things to do. I don't know what time I'll get back from that. I can't just pick up and move. I have a life." I knew I couldn't stay in this mess, and I knew they had to go over it before it was cleaned up. Reality just hadn't quite made it from my brain to my mouth. I gave myself a mental "shut up." A hotel was expensive and maybe not an option on short notice, and the airport customer had a plane to catch.

"And what about Belle?" What about Belle? When had she become my responsibility? And when had I become Jon's responsibility?

"I have a whole house. I'm sure we can fit Belle in somewhere." Jon put his hand out toward me.

"You have a house? How many bedrooms? How many bathrooms? Who else lives there? I don't know enough about you to move in. And Belle! She'll go through the roof. She can barely be in the same room with a cop."

"Calm down." Jon held my hand and started to massage it.

"Belle had no problem moving in with you. She's going to like my kitchen a lot better. I have three bedrooms and two bathrooms. I just want to get a handle on where Scarpelli comes into this. Belle didn't shoot Horace and he didn't shoot himself. Honey, a guy is dead. Someone killed him. And Belle is a witness to something, even if she doesn't know what. I need to keep an eye on you because …" He stopped talking and looked at me. "Well, just because. I'm not sure why." He ran his hand up my arm. I was considering my response when the thumping of feet on the stairs told us the crime scene was about to be investigated. Jon went to the door. I stood there like an idiot, rubbing my hand.

"I need to pack a few things," I mumbled. I hoped I had a few things left to pack. Taxi drivers frequently carry oversize bags as standard equipment. I kept one handy in case I didn't want to drive home between late night drop-offs and early pick ups. Belle, in her previous profession, had kept the same kind of bag.

I looked disconsolately at the toothpaste. It had been used to spell out shit happens on the floor. It looked like slut opens.

"What do you think that says?" I asked Jon.

Jon looked down. "Slap happy?"

"Slut shopping?" I giggled, beginning to melt down.

"I have toothpaste in both guest rooms," Jon said. "Let's run it by Belle. You can follow me home and leave for the airport from my house. And I have a really nice shower." Jon steered me out the door.

I sighed and started down the stairs. Maybe Belle would be fine as long as she didn't have to go back to Hampshire Heights. Gunshots were part of everyday living in Hamp Heights, and the cops wouldn't get called until it was too late to catch the shooter if they got called at all.

When we got to Cool Rides, Willie, Belle and Mona were sitting around the table. Belle was humming. From the tune, and from Willie's expression, I guessed she was relating her impromptu performance in the chapel. Mona was smiling. Well, maybe.

Belle nudged Willie. "Come on, sing it." She stood up and waved her hands in the air, and they harmonized the chorus. Holy cow, I thought, she might convince them to join her at the chapel.

Jon applauded. I had other things on my mind. Like Jon Jon's house, the bedrooms in Jon's house. There was a new body in the morgue. I didn't want mine, or Belle's, or anyone's, to join it.

Willie and Mona moved to the office. Jon and I replaced them at the table. Belle stayed where she was.

Jon explained why I was still covered with soda and what had happened to my apartment and what we, or at least Jon, had decided to do about it. Belle grinned. Apparently, her cop phobia wasn't real deep.

"A real kitchen? When can we go shopping? Let's see now, I'm going to need …" She started a list of groceries. "What kind of cookware did you say you had? Oh, sorry about your apartment. I know a good cleaning service if you need it." She walked off talking to herself about ingredients and recipes.

"There's a shower in the garage. It's not pretty, but I'll use it," I grumbled. "Maybe I can pick up a few short hauls before the airport and make some money to buy those 'eat me' thongs I saw downtown," I said, looking at Jon. He had his cop face on, but I saw a flicker at the word thong. If he and Belle bonded over groceries, he might get more information that she didn't know she had.

I had an interior sigh moment. "I'll head over to your house after my airport." Jon gave me directions, and he and Belle left.

When I walked out of the shower/locker room/changing room, Mona handed me a pickup slip.

"O'Grady's bar, going to Holyoke. You're up. You have plenty of time before the airport if you hustle."

I headed out, figuring work would take my mind off reality. Normally I would avoid O'Grady's, the local bar most likely to appear in the police report. But most of their incidents take place around closing when the hard-core patrons are tossed out. Since it was early afternoon, I could look the fare over first. If it was a candidate for the barf bag, I'd keep driving and call Mona. She could hand it off to the other cab company. When a fare looked fall-down drunk, we would call the competition and pretend we were the pickup. They never said no to a fare.

As I drifted by the entrance to O'Grady's, I noticed a man, maybe midthirties, suit and tie, nice haircut. Maybe stopping for a drink after work. I pulled over and he got in.

"Where to?" I asked, punching the GPS on.

"Just get on Route 5. I'll direct you."

Route 5 had been the main road before the interstate was built. Now it's a quiet back road dotted with dead and dying businesses. A lot of life around Northampton is defined by "before the interstate went in." The interstate opened up a corridor for the transportation of people, goods and services of all kinds.

O'Grady's is about 30 feet from Route 5. I had settled into driving when my passenger said, "Take the next right."

It was a narrow side road. I swung in and there was a house hiding behind the trees on a circular drive.

"Pull in here." he said and leaned back to dig out his wallet. A big guy, dressed in a black suit and looking like an undertaker, came out of the house and started around the front of the car. That didn't look right to me. Most people who are greeting someone open the passenger door. If they mean to pay for the fare, they lean in the front passenger window. I'd lowered that window in anticipation when the man came out of the house. My passenger had his door open and one foot out. I watched the big guy pass in front of my car. He slid his hand into his jacket. He was around the car and had one hand on my door. By my door, I mean the one he would drag me out of if he intended to shoot me with the gun that he now held in his other hand.

I yanked my foot off the brake and smashed it down on the accelerator. The car lurched forward. My passenger hadn't quite cleared the door. His left leg was still in the cab and his right hand was resting on the window. The bozo at my door held on to the handle. He was big enough to stop most people with one hand. A car is not a person. And he was not going to stop 2,000 pounds of steel with 135 pounds of freaked-out woman behind the wheel.

The driveway ran out to the road between two huge pine trees. In another life I might have thought "Christmas trees." Right now I was thinking that the fastest way out was between those honkin' big trees. I knew there was room for the car, but the attached bodies hadn't noticed the trees. They were focused on holding on to the car and their guns and staying upright and getting me out of the car. I was focused on making sure they didn't do any of that. We hit the trees going 10 miles an hour. That's really slow if you're driving in traffic, but when an unprotected body, moving at that speed, hits a stationary object, it's plenty fast. The passenger-side door slammed against the tree, closing tightly on the body wedged between it and the car. The guy holding on to the driver's-side door threw out his arm to ward off the collision and ended up looking like Wyle E. Coyote in a Road Runner cartoon. I reached the end of the driveway. The backseat passenger was pinned by the door, half out of the car.

"Gaaahhh!" I heard a moan from the backseat.

"I think my arm is broken … and my leg."

"Out," I screeched. The guy hurled himself out and lay flat on the ground. I laid rubber. The back door slammed closed with the momentum of my departure.

What the hell did they want? Cabbies never carry much cash. Maybe they didn't know that.

I swung out onto the highway. About five minutes down the road my hands started to shake. Shaky hands are not good. I pulled over and leaned my head back. Shit! I threw the door open and vomited.

Now I had to go back to my apartment and brush my teeth and ... no to the apartment. I had my toothbrush with me, but no toothpaste. I needed strong toothpaste. I let my stomach settle, gripped the steering wheel with white knuckles and headed back to Northampton.

I stopped at the drugstore on the strip. My stomach was woozy, but my head had cleared, sort of. I swallowed a few times and went in. Grabbing toothpaste and a bottle of water, I zipped through the checkout without opening my mouth. No need to knock out the salesperson with vomit breath. I drank most of the water and headed back to Cool Rides.

There would be no way to avoid explaining what had happened when Willie saw the car door. I could make up some lie about a hit-and-run, but I knew that if Willie didn't figure it out, Jon would. I could lie with the best of them, but Jon had probably had some experience with the best liars in the world. I didn't have any fare money to hand over to Mona. That would make an explanation mandatory. Fares that fail to pay are a fact of every taxi driver's life. The addition of violence is less frequent but not unusual. If we reported every episode to the police, we'd spend half our waking hours in the cop-house interview room. I'd had enough of that depressing room for a long time. Willie would fix the dent in-house, and the insurance company would never hear about it. But this incident was serious enough to make me think Jon might have to know about it.

I pulled into Cool Rides. Willie and Mona were out front washing one of the cars. No one keeps cars as clean as the Cool Rides crew. And now there was mine. Two bullet holes, three dents and a big smear of dark red-brown stuff down the passenger window. I should be happy there weren't some fingers stuck in the door. Actually, I hadn't checked.

I needed normal fares. I was still shaky from the mugging and didn't want to burst into tears or throw up again. That would not impress the boss.

The damage was clearly in view. Mona and Willie stopped scrubbing and stared at the door.

"I'm okay," I said. "And the door still works, but I could use some of that cleaner." I grabbed the towels and the spray bottle and started working on the brown streak. Jon would have had a fit, but I wasn't going to press charges against those bozos. I never wanted to see them again. So evidence wasn't in my vocabulary at the moment. Drive to the airport were the words I wanted to hear.

"What the hell happened?" Willie knelt in front of the dent in the door. He stroked his hands over the damage like someone feeling a wound in a loved one.

"I'm okay," I repeated.

"We can see that," said Mona. "Don't avoid the question."

"I had a run-in with some thugs. But they look worse than me. They even look worse than the car." And maybe I'll never pick up at O'Grady's again, I thought.

"Nothing looks worse than the car." Willie continued to caress the dent.

"Well, yes, these guys do. One of them probably has a broken arm and maybe a leg, too. The other one may have a broken nose ... or face ... or body. He kind of looked flat, sort of attached to the tree."

"What tree?" Willie finally stood up and noticed me.

"Unh, the ones that they ran into, but the car didn't ... very much. I mean, just the door. Because it was open. Because he had his arm and leg out the door. Because he was trying to get out ... of the door." I stammered to a stop.

"Who?" Willie looked at me like I had an alien sticking out of my head.

"The fare. Can we go inside and discuss this?" My legs felt rubbery and I wanted to sit down. And I wanted to be allowed to drive to the airport.

We sat and I explained the disaster in Holyoke. I had no evidence that this was anything more than a mugging. I didn't recognize either of my assailants. We always keep $50 in change in the box, and it was reasonable for them to think a driver could have more than that. Muggings were unusual for us but not out of the question.

Willie sat back. "Jon stopped by and told me about the apartment. There's just too much dangerous stuff going on right now. I want you to limit your driving to airport runs with fares that we know and car service with our regulars."

I almost hugged him. Local car service was a good deal. We rented the car and driver out for $50 an hour. The customers were mostly older and had given up driving. We would run errands and take them to appointments. Sometimes we took their pets to the vet's office. It was a guaranteed $25 an hour for the driver. Combined with airport runs, it would be a respectable income. And I wouldn't have to worry about large stupid men with guns.

"Do the 7-o'clock run to the airport. That's Professor Brant. He's been out in California, so he'll be tired when he gets in. Let him sleep," Willie said.

"And Iggi Paluska wants his cat taken to the vet tomorrow. You can do that." Mona pointed to the damaged car. "Use that one. No sense in messing up one of the clean ones."

"Take the pocket limo to the airport," Willie said. We have one cab with extra-dark tinted windows and plush leather seats. It's a Scion and we all know it's not a limousine. Willie says it's a matter of attitude. And the pocket limo has attitude."

"Aawright!" I said and pulled a fist. I almost floated into the bathroom to brush my teeth.

"Good idea," said Mona. "Your breath could put another dent in that car."

For the next hour, I cleaned and detailed the cars. Maintenance is big at Cool Rides. Cars are checked at the end of each shift for the detritus that passengers leave behind. We have a collection of gloves, hats and glasses and the mysterious single shoe that means someone left with one bare foot. I found a state-police evidence envelope once, still full. Boxes of condoms, baggies of illegal substances and, once, a 2-week-old baby. When we tracked down the mother, she whined over the phone, "I just needed a break from all the crying. I knew where to find him when I was ready to pick him up." When we told her we charged $50 an hour for use of the cab, she arrived in five minutes and indignantly retrieved her squalling youngster. After that,

Willie made us check the cars after each fare. As I was finishing vacuuming the last car, Mona came out with a fare slip.

"He's going home." She grinned and handed me the yellow Post-it. The name on it was Steinberger. No address, no phone, no destination. We all knew Mr. Steinberger. He either needed a ride to or from the liquor store. Another windows-down, air-conditioner-on kind of guy, depending on how much he'd consumed before he got picked up.

He looked functional today, but when he leaned over to pick up his bag, he got stuck. I sighed, hopped out of the taxi, and grabbed the bag.

"It's really heavy. Sorry," he said.

"Unh, what's in this?" I grunted. There was a cardboard box inside the bag and a plastic bag inside the box.

"Wine."

"I don't know that much about wine." But I had never seen it packaged in a cardboard box before.

"This is really cheap. I call it booze in a box. It's awful."

"Oh," I said. "Good for cooking, I guess."

"Oh, no, we're having dinner guests. I'm serving it to them. God, I'd never drink this stuff myself."

"They like the cheap stuff?"

"No, but I'll get them stoned on cheap scotch before dinner."

"You don't like these people, do you?"

"Not especially, no."

I pulled up in front of his apartment house, two blocks from the liquor store. I waited until he'd made it inside. He'd been known to take a header over a sidewalk crack.

I returned to Cool Rides and finished detailing the mini-limo.

At 6:15, I left for the airport. When I got back, Mona was leaving for the night.

"Take the bang and dent for Iggi Paluska's cat to the vet at 10 tomorrow morning. Then I'll see if we got anything else you can't screw up."

"The bang and dent" was the new name for the car I usually drove. I didn't argue that none of the dents were my fault. I just wanted to get over to Jon's house and find out what the sleeping arrangements were going to be.

I knew Jon's house, although Jon didn't know that I knew it. Right after he'd busted me and I suddenly had access to a car because he'd taken me to Willie to get a job, I had done a little bit of semi-stalking. I wasn't sure whether I wanted to burn the house down with him in it or knock on the door and ask if he was busy for the evening. Either result would have been his fault, because he'd busted me.

The house was a beautiful, old Victorian two family side-by-side that needs some fixing up, which Jon was doing on the installment plan. Apparently he rented out the other side.

I had no doubt that Willie or Mona had already told Jon about the incident in Holyoke. He's a cop and he's a guy, so I was prepared for the control-issue thing. At the moment, I didn't feel like answering questions or justifying my job or fighting over who was in charge. I just wanted to go to bed.

The door was jerked open before I had a chance to knock. Jon stood there in jeans, work shirt and bare feet. My brain said wow, but my libido was like the piece of extra luggage the airline had lost, and I couldn't be bothered to find it. My adrenaline had spiked so many times today that I was running on nothing. I stepped back defensively.

He stepped forward and pulled me into his arms. No questions, no wandering hands. I struggled not to feel needy. I hate people who are emotional black holes. It isn't always easy for me not to be the same.

"When did you talk to Willie?" I mumbled into his chest. I wanted to know how much of my life they had shared.

"I told him about the apartment. He was upset." He paused.

"At least it wasn't the car," I said.

"And he told me about what happened in Holyoke. To the car. I assume you were in it at the time. We need to talk about you picking up strange men. Didn't your mother tell you not to do that?"

"It's my job. Besides, all men are strange."

"I know." I didn't care which of the statements he was agreeing with.

He wrapped me in big strong arms again. I leaned again. He wasn't taking this lightly, but he wasn't pressuring me. He knew I was going to stick with my job and Cool Rides.

My brain began to drift toward off. The man of my dreams and I'm so tired I'm passing out. He herded me inside and sat me on a sofa that made mine look like a dollhouse miniature.

"Belle made food. Sit, I'll get some." He went into the kitchen.

We were stuffing ourselves with macaroni salad laced with sweet peppers, sweeter onions, bacon and hard-boiled eggs when Belle made her entrance. She was dressed in blue jeans and a white sparkle top that dipped as low as it could without everything overflowing. Her shoes were ankle-breaking tall, and rhinestone earrings whacked her shoulders. She took denim to a whole new level. Boy, do I want to look like that when I grow up.

"Honey, I'm glad you like the food, but if I had that man looking at me like that, the food ain't what I'd be eating." She whirled by in a cloud of perfume. I looked over at Jon. She was right. There was an odd look in his eyes. I wasn't sure it was what Belle thought it was, though. More likely, he wanted information about the Wyle E. Coyote flat guy in Holyoke. The one with the big gun.

"I'm going out." Belle announced.

"Whoa, wait a minute. You're here because it's safe. And I don't want you doing anything that I have to explain to my boss tomorrow morning. There's a curfew in this house." Jon stood up and tried to tower over her. Given the addition of the spiked heels to Belle's 6 feet, it was a hopeless effort.

"Isn't he just the cutest thing in the world? Darlin', nobody tells Belle when to come home. Even Horace didn't try that." Belle touched Jon on the cheek with one perfectly manicured, 2-inch-long, iridescent red fingernail and kept walking toward the door. Jon might have admired Belle's swinging rear end, but he seemed more intent on getting her under his control. I admired her fingernails. And her toenails. And her shoes. And her ability to stay upright in them.

"Where the hell are you going?" Jon glanced at the handcuffs lying on the counter. His gun was probably stashed somewhere, too. Of course, Belle was carrying her big bag and she might have had a gun stuffed in it somewhere with ammo for added weight. I hoped she couldn't find it. I also wasn't sure that Jon could actually wrestle her to the floor and cuff her, despite his physical attributes.

Belle grinned wickedly. "Oh, don't get your thong in a crack. There's a late concert at the Iron Horse music hall. A friend of mine is singing. I promised her a month ago that I would be her date. She's picking me up and dropping me off." We heard a horn honk outside.

Belle had her hand on the door handle. "And tomorrow morning I'll be leaving early for choir practice." She closed the door behind her. Belle knew how to make an exit. Jon stood with his mouth shut tight.

"Choir? Do they know what they're in for? Jesus. How do I get involved with these people?" He flopped down next to me. I yawned and leaned my head against him.

I don't remember falling asleep. I don't remember Belle coming home. I don't remember Jon moving me from the couch to one of the spare bedrooms. But I opened my eyes in a strange bed. One with superhigh-thread-count cotton sheets and huge pillows. Alone.

Chapter 9

I smelled coffee and bacon. Takeout pastry, with chocolate or butter or both, is my usual breakfast. I recognized the smell of bacon because BLT is also part of my food vocabulary.

I wandered into the kitchen. Jon was standing at the counter drinking coffee and shaking aspirin out of a plastic bottle.

Belle emerged from the bathroom and sauntered into the kitchen. Her makeup was toned down, she was wearing a plain white shirt and black slacks and her shoes only added an inch to her height. They had some glitter on them, so she still made a little bit of a statement. Jon narrowed his eyes. His fingers toyed with the pair of handcuffs that still lay on the counter.

"Sweetie, how would it look if you tried to stop a woman from her God-given right to worship?" She slid the sugar bowl over and moved the cuffs down the counter, out of Jon's reach. "Add some of this to that coffee. It'll sweeten you right on up."

"Black, and you might make me doubt that there is a God." he mumbled but didn't reach for the handcuffs.

Belle swung her butt to the door. She turned. "Siiing, sing out loud." She screeched and slammed the door behind her. Jon held his head. He downed the aspirin and took a careful sip of coffee.

"Headache?"

"I didn't sleep well." Maybe because he'd slept alone, I thought to myself.

"I did. Thanks for the bed. Temporarily. I wasn't sure about the sleeping arrangements."

"I have three bedrooms. That's the sleeping arrangement ... for the moment." He looked at me wolfishly. "If you want to change that, let me know. I'm a very accommodating guy."

"No 'honey, I have a headache'?" I slid onto the seat across the counter from him.

"Honey, where you're concerned, a bullet in the brain wouldn't slow me down." He focused his blue eyes on mine. I blinked first.

"So, you want to talk about it?" he asked.

"About your headache?"

"Yesterday. The thugs. Remember? You got mugged by two big guys who are paying dearly for underestimating your blind luck." He swallowed the black coffee and winced. Belle had added chicory.

"Oh, those guys. It's a hazard of the job. Willie put me on local car service and known airport for a while. I think I can handle that."

"I want a description."

"Well, local service runs are mostly old people without driver's licenses ..." My voice trailed off when I noticed that Jon was eyeing the handcuffs again. He looked back at me.

"Just dreaming about you in handcuffs. Where at least I could keep some small amount of control over your disasters."

"Are we back to discussing sleeping arrangements?"

If looks could kill, his made a gun unnecessary.

"Okay, maybe not. The pickup looked like a stockbroker. The other guy was an oversize hockey player in a suit ... with a gun ... pointed at my head. It was hard to concentrate on detail. When I left, he was kind of flat. The stockbroker guy was rolling around on the ground holding his shoulder ... or his knee or both. You might want to check the emergency rooms."

Jon stared at me. Then he burst out laughing.

"You are truly a wonder. Let's talk about the house. Where was it?"

"In Holyoke off Route 5. He wouldn't give me an address. I'm driving along and suddenly he said, 'Turn here.'"

"Could you find it again?"

"In a heartbeat."

"We have to go there."

"Right now? I have an airport run in a couple hours."

"Right after your run." His cell phone rang and he snatched it off the counter where he'd laid it next to the handcuffs.

"Stevens. What?" He listened for 10 seconds. "What?" he yelled into the phone. "Yeah, give me the location. I can be there in 10."

I inched closer, hoping to overhear the other end of the conversation. Jon's hand came up and covered my face completely, keeping me from hearing anything. He snapped the phone closed and moved his hand over to my cheek and down my neck. He pulled me over and kissed me lightly on the lips. Then he kissed me harder and deeper and our tongues got involved and … ummm.

When we came up for air his eyes were dark and thoughtful. He kissed my nose and said, "You're on your own. I need to get to the station." He went to a small closet just inside the front door and extracted his holster and gun. After checking the gun, he clipped it to his belt and shrugged into a jacket that had been hanging in the closet. He headed toward the door.

"Wait, what's going on? This is Northampton. Are we having a crime wave?" I figured he would pull that need-to-know stuff and stonewall me. I was right.

"Gotta go. Be sure the door is locked when you leave. I'll call you later about checking out that house." He looked at me. "When I leave, flip the dead bolt. And be careful going out to your car. Don't hang around. Okay?" He handed me a key. "This is for the front door." He was giving me a key to his house. Jon is any straight woman's wet dream, and maybe some not-so-straight ones and, most likely, all the not-so-straight men. I stared at the key for two seconds.

"Is there something you need to tell me? On a need-to-know basis, sometimes I need to know." Like right now. My voice went up an octave.

"No," he replied. His cell phone rang again. He snapped it open and listened for another 10 seconds. "Oh, shit. No surprise. Yeah, okay, I'll tell her. Send someone over to keep an eye out. Thanks." He closed it slowly and looked at me.

"That was Rodriguez at the station. The press has the story. You'll see it in the paper anyway." He turned away from me and looked out the window.

"What, what? Did something happen at Cool Rides? Is everyone okay? Where is Belle? What's going on?" I was yelling by this point, and Jon grabbed me by the shoulders.

"Calm down. It's no one you know. I got another body. That crazy lady lawyer lost her husband."

"Oh, no, she didn't shoot him somewhere besides in the butt, did she?"

"She was in court with about 30 other people, including a judge and jury, when he was killed. We have a witness who heard the shots. Didn't see anything, but at least we have a real time of death. Shit! I don't know what to do with you." He scowled, which seemed to be a common expression for him these days. "I want you to stay in very public places until we figure out what the hell is going on. I know Scarpelli is connected. I need to figure it out before we find any more bodies."

"I have that airport run anyway." There isn't any place with more security these days than an airport. For a taxi driver, airport security can be an inconvenient pain in the backside. Right now, it was fine with me. I just had to pick up the fare and get him there first. And I would have Belle with me.

"Then I'll see you tonight. Don't go anywhere that there aren't lots of people. Safe rides only, okay?"

"Humph," I answered.

And he left me sitting there, alone, in his house. What kind of fool was he? I had some time before I picked up the airport run. I started with the master bedroom.

His bed was king size. A huge painting of a peach hung on the wall opposite the bed. The peach managed to resemble something erotically, sexually feminine and still look like a peach. His bedroom closet had … my God, the man owned a tuxedo. It was in a clear cleaner's bag so it might have been used recently. Not in Northampton. Now I had to wonder where Jon might wear a tux.

Nothing weird in the bedside table. Nothing dangerous in the medicine cabinet. Master bath was amazing. The shower was a walk-in with a built-in shelf, big enough to sit on. Jon in the shower flicked through my mind.

There was a sound system in the living room with lots of DVDs. The TV was a large flat-screen. The couch could accommodate two horizontal or six vertical.

The food in the fridge was fresh, indicating that Belle had just bought it. The kitchen was beautiful, with lots of pots and pans, mostly unused.

A basement can represent a major philosophical statement or it can be a dumping ground. Jon's was a statement. It had more carpentry tools than the kitchen had cooking tools, and these looked well used. I headed back upstairs.

He didn't have any sex toys, women's underwear or even condoms in his house, so I figured he wasn't involved with anyone.

With an hour before my first scheduled pickup, I could see whether there were any short hauls I could squeeze in for extra money. Or I could satisfy more of my curiosity.

Curiosity won. I decided to see if Jon's renter in the other half of the house was a hot babe who kept all the sex toys on her side. Or maybe a hot guy and I could forget all about Jon. I was pretty sure Jon wasn't gay, but I was always up for meeting a hot guy.

I looked out the front door to check for bad guys. The street was empty. Mailboxes were side by side on the porch. Stevens was painted in white on a plain black box. The other box was a cute birdhouse with Emmy Lucille Streeter painted on it.

I rang the doorbell. I hadn't decided what I was going to say if a blond bombshell opened the door.

It was my ash-lady airport run. She must have scattered Grandpa's ashes in record time. It didn't seem very long since I'd dropped her off. I pictured her dumping the cardboard box under a rock at a highway rest stop outside an airport in Anywhere, USA.

The overwhelming smell of baking cookies wafted out the door.

"May I help you?" She smiled beatifically at me.

"Uhh, I'm staying next door temporarily, and I, uh, thought it might be nice to meet the neighbors." And find out what she looked like and how much she knew about Jon. "My name is Honey."

"Oh, how nice. I'm Lucille. Are you providing sexual favors for Jon while you're staying there? He's such a nice young man."

I could have said, "No, but if you have any suggestions, I'm all ears." But I decided to keep Jon's sexual life out of the conversation. "Those cookies smell wonderful. Are you baking them yourself?"

"Oh, yes. I use them to attract the cute men at the senior center. Would you care to try one? You could give me an opinion about how lucky I might get."

"Thanks. I can't stay long, though. I drive for Cool Rides Taxi and I have a pickup at 10." I glanced behind me as I stepped through the door, just to see if Jon's request for someone to keep an eye out had been taken seriously. The only car on the block was a black Lincoln that had just pulled up, and the suits inside were not police officers. I moved to a window and peered out to get a better look at the passenger who was leaning his arm out the car window. It had a cast on it. I couldn't see his face.

"Why, who would that be? What an impressive car." Granny had moved up behind me.

"Those aren't very nice guys. I think maybe they tried to mug me yesterday." The one leaning out the window moved his oversize arm. His head came into view. By this time I'd nicknamed my attackers Bozo and Bongo. I recognized Bozo's black-and-blue face.

"Really? Well, don't you worry, dear. We women take care of ourselves. I have just the solution." She disappeared into the kitchen and came back with a huge gun in her hand.

"No! Absolutely not. No guns," I squeaked.

"Oh, sweetie. Jon keeps telling me to call any time I have any problems, but, you know, I've always been independent. I really do like to take care of myself. And I do believe I'm a better shot than Jon anyway. Shall we find out? I think I can nail that tire from here." She opened the curtain and took aim. Boom, pop! The sound inside the house was deafening. I jumped back from the window.

"I really need to get a silencer for this gun," said Lucille.

The arm jumped inside the car, the window rolled up and the car skidded down the street. They didn't return fire. In half a block, their tire started to deflate with a kerthump, kerthump. They pulled over. Guess they didn't have run-flats. Run-flat tires only handle marginally better than a tire with a bullet hole in it.

"I think it's cookie time," Granny said and headed off toward the kitchen. I continued to watch the car for a second, shrugged, and followed her. "I was the best shot on the firing range, you know." She tucked the gun into the back of the kitchen junk drawer.

Firing range? Where did Jon get his tenants? Then I noticed the framed photos and certificates on the wall. One of the pictures was of a younger Lucille with Vice President Gore. She was wearing a badge and a jacket, both with FBI in large, very clear letters. The certificate next to it was one for achievement on the firing range. Nice neighbor. Handy to have around if someone is trying to knock you off.

I was on my second cookie when the doorbell rang. We both jumped a little, but Granny got up and peeked out the window.

"Oh my, aren't we having the best visitors today? It's Officer Rodriguez. We have cookies, dear," she said and opened the door.

The uniformed officer stepped in and eyed the cookies.

"What's with the suits down the street? They're changing the tire on that big Lincoln. They looked nervous when I drove by. You wouldn't know anything about that would you?" he asked.

"Why, dear, Honey and I have just been enjoying these freshly made chocolate chip cookies." Granny pushed the cookie plate closer.

"Oh gosh, look at the time. I have an airport pick up in 10 minutes." I headed for the door. Rodriguez was right behind me.

"I'll just make sure everything is locked up." He smiled. "Lieutenant's orders."

I glanced down the street, zipped in, got my bag, locked up and was backing the cab out of the driveway when the patrol car pulled up behind me.

I drove slowly to the end of the block, taking care to wave at the guy changing the tire. He looked up as I drove by. His face was a mask of bruises with a bandage across the nose. He held up a finger as I drove by and dropped it quickly as the patrol car followed.

Chapter 10

When I pulled into Cool Rides, the patrol car continued by, leaving me in the very public hands of a busy transportation service. Belle was waiting for me.

"How was choir practice?"

"I might have to start believing in God." She had added some makeup to her face and changed into sparkle and spandex. Black leather heels now added 3 inches to her formidable height. "Mona says I'm riding with you to the airport and then to meet Iggi Paluska."

We headed out to pick up the airport fare. We would pick up Iggi when we got back. The airport is an hour and a half round trip, so we were calling it a little close, but with two people, one could lug bags and open doors while the other did car control and collected money.

I drove to the North Prince Motel, on the outskirts of town. We usually pick up airport runs from in-town hotels. North Prince catered to a lower-income clientele that didn't usually travel far enough to need an airplane.

I saw the flashing lights from a long way away. As we got closer to the motel, I realized the cop cars were in the motel parking lot. And there were lots of them. Including Jon's nondescript police-issued clunker.

Belle looked at me. "Honey, I think maybe we could turn around here. I'm pretty sure I just got an allergic reaction to this taxi-driving stuff."

"You're not allergic to taxi driving. It's the cop cars. We'll just pick up our fare and leave."

I pulled out my fare slip. The name written on it was Mr. Smith. Well, there are a lot of real Mr. Smiths in the world. I looked at the unit number that Mona had jotted down. Number 5. Unfortunately, number 5 was occupied by a lot of police officers, probably none of them named Mr. Smith. As I thought about how to find out if I still had an airport run, Jon turned and spotted the cab. Then he saw me. He jammed his fists in his pockets and walked slowly to the taxi.

"Don't tell me." He leaned against the passenger door. Belle tried to sink lower. "What's the name of your fare?"

I stared at my feet and mumbled the name. I knew my fare was a no-show. Sort of. "I don't have a fare, do I?" I asked mournfully.

Belle sunk as low as she could in the seat. Six feet of female with another few inches of Afro is hard to hide in a Scion XB or, for that matter, in a tractor trailer.

"We'll talk later." Jon shook his head and strode back to the crime scene. On the upside, we wouldn't be late picking up Iggi Paluska. I turned the cab around and headed back toward town.

Iggi Paluska was a regular user of our car service. Today's trip was to the hospital for blood tests and then back to his house to pick up his cat and truck it to the vet. I drove, with Belle riding shotgun. Once she knew his errand pattern, she could pick him up by herself.

At 88, Iggi had given up his car. This was good because he had a lot of memory lapses. Like where he lived and what he'd done yesterday.

I parked in the driveway. The garage door slid up. Iggi stood at the top of a long wooden ramp, backlighted by the windows in the house. His dogs set up a howl as the door closed. He pushed his walker down the ramp.

"Sure knows how to make an entrance," Belle said. She unfolded herself out of the car and opened the door for him.

"Hey, chicky, you the new driver?" Iggi looked Belle over as she loaded his walker behind the seat and set his oxygen tank on the floor between his feet.

"You bet. I'm gonna show this crew what real driving is about. I could do stunts for The Italian Job." Belle smiled.

We got to the hospital, dropped Iggi at the entrance and went off to run his errands. When we returned, the nurse said Iggi had finished and left. We circled the hospital until we found him at an unused side entrance, carefully studying a blank wall.

As Belle got out to help Iggi, a black Lincoln town car slid up behind the cab. Bozo, surprisingly nimble for a man with his arm in a cast, jumped out, wrapped his fist in Belle's hair and yanked her toward the Lincoln. Iggi, sensing that this was not on the agenda, raised his walker and charged after Belle. Except he forgot about the oxygen tank. It spilled off his walker, tubes trailing, and rolled toward Bozo and Belle. Bozo saw movement out of the corner of his eye. He pulled his gun and fired off a shot, missing the target but hitting the tire of his car. Belle planted her feet and pulled back. Bozo stumbled and dropped his gun. It fired off another bullet, which hit the release valve on Iggi's oxygen tank. The tank took off like a rocket, blasting around the parking lot like it was in a pinball machine. Belle jumped sideways as it whistled by her legs. It hit Bozo's foot and flipped him onto his back. His head hit the pavement. The oxygen tank zinged off the rear bumper of the Lincoln, bounced off the fender of the cab and sailed straight up in the air. It turned a graceful arc, shot back down like an armor-piercing bullet, and stopped, stuck, valve down, in the roof of the Lincoln. It fizzed out the last of the oxygen and stayed put.

Belle stuffed Iggi into the backseat of the cab, barreled into the front, and yelled, "Drive!"

I nailed it up the hill and out of the parking lot, looking back long enough to see Bozo lying on the ground with his leg sticking out at an ugly angle. The last I thing I saw was Bongo trying to get Bozo into the Lincoln. I hoped they forgot to replace the spare tire.

"Hey, you guys are a lot more fun than Willie, but I think I have to add a new oxygen tank to my shopping list. You know those guys?" Iggi looked at Belle. His breathing was a little heavy.

"Unh, not really. Maybe friends of Honey's?"

"Nope!" I replied to Iggi's questioning look.

I glanced at him in the rearview mirror. He was grinning from ear to ear, but his breath had started a wheezy, sucky sound. The oxygen tank definitely needed to be our next stop. I headed out North Prince Street to the medical-supply store.

Now I'd have to decide how much, if any, of this stuff I should tell Jon, who, being a cop, would act like a cop. Belle wouldn't tell him anything. Iggi Paluska would forget it before we got his new oxygen tank.

If I told the police about Bozo and Bongo stalking me or Belle, Jon would have a patrol car on my tail. That would seriously cramp my style and cut into my tips. And I didn't want to squeal on Granny. I didn't know whether Jon even knew she had a gun. I was sure that Officer Rodriguez had told him about the guys changing a tire near the house. Why volunteer to tell him why the tire needed to be changed?

This time they had gone straight for Belle, so I figured I wasn't as important to them. They had made their move when a quiet opportunity presented itself, which meant they were watching us. I didn't think anyone had witnessed the hospital attack, because no one came to the rescue and no police arrived. If I reported this to Jon, he might slap Belle into protective custody or something equally self-defeating. I was getting to know Belle and I was sure she wouldn't react well.

We arrived at the medical-supply store and I hopped out with my charge card. I really didn't think Iggi should pay for this.

Belle beat me to the door. She had her credit card in hand as well.

"I'll get this one. Those assholes weren't after Iggi ... or you." She opened the door.

"Belle, you haven't even made any fares yet. Ever hear of cash flow?"

"Sweetie, don't you worry about Belle. I made plenty of money as a ho. I stashed some and invested most of it. Cash flow is not my current problem."

Hmmm … interesting to know.

We got Iggi's canned breath and took him home. He said he was feeling lightheaded, so I told him the cat could wait until tomorrow. I helped him make an appointment with the vet for the next morning, promising to pick up, transport, and return the cat, whose name was Ferocious.

I went back to work, taking an elderly lady to the grocery store, where she examined every can of cat food with a flashlight and magnifying glass. Belle was in a cooking mood, so she went back to Jon's house.

The elderly gentlemen had visited the porn store again and needed ride to the retirement home. They argued over who would wear a black thong that had Northampton, eat here embroidered on the crotch.

My next fare was a fiftysomething woman suffering through the change of life. She turned the air conditioning on full and fanned her face.

"Raging hormones, honey. That's what this is about. If I had a sex life, I bet this wouldn't happen. My hormones would get all used up. What I need is a young stud. And maybe a good dildo. Can't you turn the air conditioning up any higher? It's hotter than a whore's tit in here."

My teeth were chattering.

"How much you figure a good gigolo is gonna cost me? Would that be a problem in a divorce case?" She dropped the fan. "Jesus, it's cold in here. Maybe you should turn on the heat. What, is your air conditioning busted?"

Her flushed face had turned pasty white. I flipped the air off. I couldn't wait to hit 50.

When I got back to the garage, I decided to wash the car. I was rinsing it off when Jon sauntered out of the office. He was in blue jeans and a black T-shirt, with no indication that he was a cop. Belle would approve.

"Need some help?" He took the hose from my hand. I was hot and sweaty from working on the car, and my excessively curly hair was in an uproar.

Jon smiled. "I see wet T-shirts in your future."

And he held the hose over my head. I squeaked and grabbed for his hand, which he held out of reach, grinning broadly as he checked out my wet T-shirt. We looked like a couple of teenagers, wrestling for the hose until we were both soaked. Suddenly we were nose to nose and his hand was on my butt. The hose cascaded water over the car and the office window. Mona came barreling out the door just as Jon's other hand lowered itself to cup my head, changing the direction of the hose. Mona got drenched. Jon kissed me anyway.

"Aaack," Mona spluttered. "It's clean enough already. Go home!" She turned off the water at the other end of the hose.

I backed away from Jon. His eyes followed me. "I'll give you a ride to my house."

We made it to Jon's doorstep before his cell phone rang.

"Shit," he mumbled and turned away. "Yeah, okay." He brushed a stray hair out of my eyes. "I've been summoned." And turned back to his car.

I couldn't decide if I was relieved or disappointed. I hoped he had a change of clothes at the station.

"Oohwee, what was that about? And what happened to your clothes?" Belle looked at me.

"Give me dessert. I'll skip dinner." I went inside and locked the door. Jon didn't get home until sometime in the wee hours.

Belle and I left early and didn't disturb Jon. There was no sign of any bad guys.

We had to pick up Iggi Paluska's cat for a few minutes of pain and then we could bundle it back home.

The parking lot was empty at the vet's office. After 10 minutes, Belle came out with the cat slung over her shoulder and the carrying box under her arm. I was moving her oversize bag off the seat when I heard the screech of brakes. The Lincoln Town Car rocked to a stop behind the cab.

They had increased their ranks to three. The new guy was bigger but lost the intimidation factor by wearing a lopsided toupee. Bozo was at the wheel. The other two jumped out and flanked Belle. One pulled, the other pushed. Belle balked. The cat saw an escape route. He bounced off Belle, onto the toupee and dug in. The rag slid down over new guy's face. Feline claws sunk into bare flesh, launched off, and the cat slithered under the cab. Lines of blood oozed down the bald head. It was like a target. I swung Belle's purse as hard as I could and scored a direct hit. He went down like a sack of sand. The Lincoln screeched out of the parking lot with me screaming after it. Belle's foot hung out the door. Her gold shoe sparkled in the sunlight. It flipped off and flew a graceful arc onto the pavement as the car door slammed shut. A string of profanities came out of my mouth that shocked even me. I bent and picked up the shoe.

I couldn't catch up with the retreating car, so I turned back to corral the cat. The third guy was still spread-eagled in the parking lot next to the cab. I wondered what was in Belle's bag. I bound his wrists and ankles with my roll of duct tape and accidentally kicked him in the ribs. I managed to coax the cat back into its mini-house and tripped over the bald guy's head. I stepped on his leg on my way to get the cell phone to call Jon.

"Stevens."

"They got Belle. They snatched her in broad daylight, at the vet's office. But I got one of them. I hit him with Belle's bag." I was past the adrenaline rush and my speech was getting loud and chaotic. This stuff was not in my job description.

I leaned on the car and looked at the shoe in my hand. All I'd wanted was to make the rent. Belle had become a friend and I wanted to keep her. Someone was derailing my plan. Anger replaced adrenaline.

"I'm on my way. Give me a description of the car. Did you get a license?" Jon sounded unusually frantic.

By the time the first patrol car arrived, I had added more tape and the guy had gone from looking like a roped steer to something out of Cocoon. With great restraint, I left breathing space around his nose.

An hour later, I had finished giving my statement to Jon. I delivered the cat back to Iggi and we all headed home. Without Belle.

By this time, I knew Bozo well enough to identify him if the police could drag his ass into the station. Jon had seen him when we were leaving Holyoke and knew him as one of Scarpelli's goons. It was only a matter of time before they found him. If he stayed in the area and if he stayed alive. No one knew what made Belle so valuable to the Scarpellis. They seemed to want her alive, so my guess was information.

Money, drugs and guns came to mind. The guy I had dropped at the vet's office was in police custody. I hoped he would talk his toupee off.

My apartment had been cleaned, but I didn't feel like facing it right now. And Jon didn't want me wandering around by myself. I slumped on the sofa in Jon's living room. Jon paced around me.

"Jesus, this is Northampton. How can we be getting this kind of violence? Springfield is giving me a hard time about trying to find Belle. Either they aren't interested or they don't want her to be found. They told my superiors that it's a turf war and implied that she went off with a new pimp. Tell me she hasn't gone back to turning tricks."

"When would she have time to do that?" The implication that I didn't know the difference between Belle going willingly or being taken bugged me. "She's spending her nights here, days at the cab company. I refuse to believe she could be doing that kind of business out of the taxi between fares. We would notice that." I was pissy already, and Jon's question, justified though it was, sent me over the edge. I stomped off to my assigned bedroom.

Chapter 11

In the morning, Jon was gone. I stuck my head in the fridge. Nothing there. God, I missed Belle. I decided to go to the 7/11 for some orange juice. And some donuts. And some coffee.

The 7-Eleven clerk was restocking shelves. He was dancing to the iPod noise streaming into his ears. I walked to the big cooling unit in the back. Another customer was head in, rear out of the fridge. I had seen that butt before. Shit! Bozo! I should have called the cops, but rage short-circuited my brain. I went straight for revenge. I snuck up as quietly as sneaker-sucking floors allow. The glass door reflected his face. It didn't look good. Black eyes. Band-Aid on his nose. I slammed the door on his head. He went to his knees. I grabbed a box of ice cream and hit him in the face. Then I grabbed a gallon of milk. Then I grabbed a bottle of soda. I was out of control. His eyes were wide and glazed. A can of Cheez Whiz somehow ended up in my hand. I sprayed his face. I wonder what's in Cheez

Whiz. He screamed and flipped over backward into a shelf of ancient Twinkies. His feet slid on the Twinkies and he landed headfirst on the floor. My rage began to fade as I fished out my duct tape.

By the time Jon got there, I had calmed myself down. I had calmed the clerk down and helped him restock the Twinkie shelf. I had bought the OJ and the extra-hard ice cream and a package of doughnuts. I had recapped the Cheez Whiz and put it back on the shelf.

"Honey." Jon nodded to me. He looked around the 7-Eleven. "You're depleting Scarpelli's ranks."

I looked down. "I got some orange juice and doughnuts. In case you forgot breakfast." I paused. "And ice cream. It's too hard to eat right now."

I looked at the carton in my hand. There was a head-shaped dent in it. Maybe I didn't want it for breakfast.

"You need a ride? We need to talk," Jon said. The officers loaded Bozo into the patrol car.

"No, I have the cab. I need to go make a living. You will call me with any new developments, right?" I tried to look deeply into Jon's eyes. He was in his cop head again. All I saw was my face reflected back at me.

"We need to go find that house where they tried to take you. I don't think Scarpelli is dumb enough to use one of his own, but so far smart hasn't been his M.O." Jon said.

"I guess I could call Willie. Maybe there's nothing happening right now."

"Good," Jon said. He walked over and talked to the uniforms. One of them got in Jon's car and drove off. I called Mona.

Jon looked at me. "We have a person-of-interest warrant out on Bozo, so we can hold on to him. I don't think he's going to talk, but it's gotta piss Scarpelli off. Maybe he'll do something stupid."

Yeah, like shoot me. Jon might move me to a more secure place ... like jail.

"Mona wants me back at the office by 10. Have a doughnut," I tossed the ice cream into the trash.

We found the house on Route 5. Jon circled around it and pounded on the door. No one home, no nearby neighbors. We drove back to Northampton. Jon would run the address. He might be able to get a search warrant from a judge, but he had his hands pretty full right now and search warrants were not easy to come by. Since he had two of the goons who had grabbed Belle, the uniforms would start doing a door-to-door with their photos near the two murder scenes. Murder was, I remembered, the crime he was trying to solve. Springfield and Holyoke were pretending to cooperate with the effort to find Belle, but it was common knowledge that they had mixed feelings about Scarpelli. Some of them liked him. Some wanted to bust him. Some considered him a pillar of the community. One way or another, most of them made a living because of him. And how Belle had made a living was also common knowledge. I didn't think prostitutes were very high up on the police list of people to be grateful to.

"I'll see you tonight. Try to stay out of trouble," Jon said when I dropped him off at the station.

Humph. He was assuming that I would be at his house that night and implying that the trouble was my fault. I took my bag of breakfast and headed for Cool Rides.

Mona met me at the door. I held the doughnuts in front of me defensively.

She scowled. "I hate it when it's slow." She plopped herself into a chair. "Give me those damn doughnuts."

We ate doughnuts and looked bored. After 15 minutes I was pacing. After 20 I had eaten five doughnuts and was as bloated and grouchy as a pregnant cat.

"I'm going uptown. See what I can scare up." Susan, the crazy lady lawyer with the red shoes, had inexplicably popped into my mind. Why had she shot her husband's butt? The husband who now had a hole in his head. And how did that tie in with Horace? Or with Scarpelli? Was she still a friend of Belle's?

"Whatever," said Mona. She probably assumed I'd try to scare up some fares. I might do that, too.

I pulled up in front of the office of Susan Young, attorney at law. A bunch of miserable-looking people were sitting in front of the dentist's office, but the attorney's side was locked up tight. I drove back to Cool Rides and looked up Susan Young in the phone book. The only listing was her office. I went to the driver's pickup log, checked to see if any other drivers had picked her up at home, and there she was. Andrew had taken her from her condo to her office three weeks ago. She lived in the old jail condos on Union Street. Some enterprising developer had bought the aging county jail and converted it to very expensive condos. Sometimes the law pays well. I wondered when the city of San Francisco would see Alcatraz for its real potential. What kind of cool condos could that rock be?

Susan Young had a three-bedroom on the first floor, partially below ground. The only parking space was between an aging Volvo and a Lincoln Town Car. I parked the cab around the corner.

I rang Susan's bell and waited. Ten seconds passed. I could hear someone on the other side of the door, but it was muffled. Good soundproofing. I waited another 10 seconds and rang again. Susan opened the door.

"Honey, what are you doing here?" She looked surprised and a little nervous.

"I just stopped by to see if you had any thoughts on Belle. You know she's been kidnapped." I leaned against the doorjamb to force her to ask me in. It didn't work.

"Now is not a good time." She didn't back up. I changed tactics.

"I could come back later." I stared at her. She shrugged.

"Call the office. Make an appointment. I really don't have time right now." Now she sounded mad.

"I'll do that." I turned and walked down the sidewalk. When I looked back, she had closed the door.

I walked around the block until I was behind the jail. There were ground-level windows on the side of the condo, hidden behind foundation plantings. I wiggled between the bushes. Bars covered the window on the inside. I looked in and saw Belle sitting with her back against the wall and her butt on the bare floor. There was no furniture. I tapped on the window. No reaction. I banged harder. Belle looked up.

She pushed herself to her feet, gesturing wildly. I couldn't hear anything. Soundproof glass? Finally I read her lips.

"Get help, stupid!"

I wiggled back out of the bushes, stood up and found myself face-to-chest with a very large man in a black suit.

"Inside." He gestured with the gun that was in his hand. We went around the corner and up the front steps to Susan's condo. He knocked and the door jerked open.

"What now?" Susan Young stood there, holding the door and looking really pissed.

"Uh, I found her at the window. The special-room window." His speech was slow. He sounded slightly off.

"Jesus Christ, you just never give up, do you?" Susan stepped back. The big guy shoved me inside. "Search her and put her in with the other stupid."

I was escorted down the hall to the bare room where Belle was sitting again, on the bare floor.

"Man, oh man. I can't believe they caught you. All you had to do was get out of here." Belle rested her head against the wall.

"Belle, what the hell is going on? What's wrong with Susan? Is Scarpelli holding her hostage?"

"You dummy." Belle sighed. "Susan is Scarpelli's kid. Like father, like daughter. Only, I'd guess, she's tryin' to run the whole show. I'm thinkin' Daddy isn't too happy."

"Susan Scarpelli? How come the cops didn't know about this?" I couldn't believe she could float right under their radar.

"Nobody knows. I only found out because one of the goons around here called her Miss Scarpelli. I'd heard through the grapevine that the old man had a daughter out on the West Coast. I guess she decided to come back and join his 'family'." She made the word sound obscene.

I was on information overload. "So what's with her husband getting whacked?"

"Turf wars?" Belle stood and went to the window. "I guess Horace got mixed up in it. He wasn't too bright sometimes."

I joined her at the window. We could see the infamous Lincoln Town Car through the bushes.

"Like between her and her dad? Why shoot Horace?"

"He had something. I don't know what. Damn. They think I know where he stashed whatever it is. The bastard must've told them I knew. Which I don't." She kicked the wall and grabbed her toe.

"Fuckin' solid walls. Shit."

I kept looking out the window. "Hey." I pointed at Susan and two of the men getting into the car.

"That means they left the idiot guy here with us." Belle paced.

"So he must have the keys to open this door. We need a plan." I pretended I had just eaten a handful of Lucille's cookies. Sugar always makes me think more clearly.

"Yeah, and he's also got a gun. A big goon gun with a big goon body. He opens that door, most likely he's gonna shoot you. Be sure you put that in your plan."

"Can he hear us through this stuff?" I pushed on the door. Solid.

"It's soundproof, so only if you scream. I found that out when I needed to go pee. Jesus, did I scream. That's the only reason he'll open the door."

Soundproof doors and barred windows required some paranoia. Susan's sanity was beginning to seem unlikely.

"He won't shoot me." I stripped off my T-shirt and handed it to Belle.

Then I dropped my jeans and lay down on the cold, hard, bare floor.

"Strangle him with the T-shirt." I spread my arms and legs. "Start screaming."

Belle stared at me for about two seconds. Then she pounded on the door and screeched, "She's trying to kill me. Heeelllppp, get her off me."

The guy who had found me at the window opened the door. He held a big gun with one of those silencer things on it. He stared at my mostly bare body. He looked like he might have a regular relationship with a bottle of steroid pills. Great for bulking up the body, but they don't do much for brain function.

"Wow!" He grinned and took a step forward. Belle was behind the door. She threw the T-shirt over his head, executioner-style, jumped on his back, and wrapped her legs around his middle. He careened around the room, arms cartwheeling the air. I jumped up, shoved my hands between his legs, grabbed something big and squishy and twisted as hard as I could.

"Aurrrgh!" he screeched. I guess the gun went off, because his foot exploded. Bellowing like a bull, he launched himself, headfirst, into the wall. And sank to the floor like a wet mop. Belle dismounted.

"Hot damn. We're outta here." She pried the gun out of his hand and snatched the key from his pocket. I grabbed my T-shirt off his head. Ugh.

"Wait." I shimmied into my jeans, rammed feet into sneakers and was about to stagger out the door. My over-size bag was sitting on the kitchen counter. I pulled out the duct tape and finished the job. I promised myself I would call Jon as soon as we were safe. Belle locked the door to the special room.

We went out the front door and raced down the steps and around the corner to the cab. Amazingly, it was still there. The keys were in my bag. No one ever said the bad guys were smart.

"Honey, you got steel nerves. I can't believe you dropped your drawers like that. I can't believe you even thought of it. Yeah, lady, steel nerves." Belle laughed and crammed herself into the passenger seat.

I giggled, "You want steel nerves, try driving down the interstate at 80 miles an hour in one of these units with an 18-wheeler on each side of you." In a Scion XB, the peripheral vision is so good that you can see the fine print on the truck next to you. I'd done early-morning runs where the night crawlers were just coming off shift and the day hoppers were joining the crowd at the same time. The road was coated with trucks of every size, shape and color. I'd gotten boxed in more than once.

I jumped in and laid rubber. I was giddy and put a little more foot into it than I needed. My mind was racing around thinking about weird things, like trucks and the interstate.

"Where do you think Susan went?" I asked Belle. I had no idea what to do. Other than our firsthand experience, we had no hard evidence that Susan was involved in anything illegal. By the time Jon got a search warrant, if he got one, the guy we left in her condo would be gone. Belle's credibility was shaky, given her previous profession. Susan was a lawyer and very slippery. I bet she had plenty of good explanations for what had happened. We decided to hole up in Jon's house while we came up with a plan.

I pulled the cab in and let the garage door down. No reason to advertise our presence. We struggled inside, our bruised bodies suffering from an emotional high that was dropping like bird shit. I sagged against the door.

"Lock everything in sight," I said to Belle. "We can go next door and see if Granny's home. At least she's got a gun."

"A gun? I had a gun. In my bag when I was snatched."

"Your bag! I've still got it." I went into the guest bedroom and came back with the oversize bag. I upended it on the kitchen counter. Shit. She had a gun, all right. And a couple of pounds of ammo to go with it. No wonder the guy at the vet's office had gone down so fast.

"Oh my, where did all that come from? The bad guys must have left it in my purse. What's a woman to do?" Belle blinked in wide-eyed wonder.

"Right. We need to get a plan together. Susan won't be happy when she gets home." I hoped she'd gone out for a long time. I unlatched the locks and peeked out the door. No action outside. I reached my hand around and knocked on Granny's door.

"Coming." I heard Granny sing out through the wall. Not as soundproof as Susan's.

"Why, hello, dearie." Granny's head popped out. We could have held our conversation door to door, but I liked her for backup. I had seen her in action. Big gun, good aim. "I have cookies." She said.

From mayhem and murder to cookies and tea. Belle and I slipped out Jon's door and through Granny's.

"Hi. We didn't really have time to meet properly before. This is Belle, and my name is Honey. How's the cookie baking? Getting lucky?"

Granny extended a hand with a smear of cookie dough across the back. "I'm Lucille. And, no, you can't call me Lucy. I'm trying a new recipe. I got lucky with the last one, but there's always room for improvement, I say. The better the cookies, the better the sex. Men will extend themselves a bit more if the rewards are great enough." She nodded her head. "Although I don't believe Jonny needs cookies to perform well."

And how would you know? I wondered.

I edged closer to the source of bliss.

"Go ahead now, take as many as you need. They may enhance your performance as well. I'll ask Jonny next time I see him. Where is he anyway? I don't see him so much anymore. I hope that means you're keeping him busy."

Oh, yeah, we're doing that.

"Cookie-enhanced sex performance?" Belle asked and snatched the platter off the table.

"Um, maybe we should give Jon a call. Let him know we're all sitting around eating cookies. That is you and me and Belle." I was hoping Lucille would call him and mention Belle. Then I wouldn't have to.

I was on my third cookie when we heard a car in the drive. I jumped.

"Nervous, dearie?" Lucille went to the window. "I know an affair with Jonny might fill me with anticipation. Oh good, it's Jonny," she said, looking out the window. "I'll just put some cookies on a plate for you to take over to him. And let me add these. I got the extra-large size. I've only seen him naked once, but Jon is well hung. He worked undercover on a male-strip-club bust. They were running a hijacking ring that specialized in stealing shipments of sex toys and selling them out of the back of the strip joint. I just happened to be in the audience one night." She handed me a package of extra-large condoms. I tried to imagine Lucille stuffing dollar bills into Jon's G-string. I was envisioning Jon as a male stripper when his front door slammed. Lucille stared off into space, maybe rerunning the picture of Jon in his stripper outfit. "Of course, sometimes they stuff socks in those stringy things. You know, to make it look more enticing." She smiled absently and patted the condoms in my hand. "But I'm pretty sure Jonny is for real." I suspected she was right, but I decided not to add to the image.

Cookies and condoms. The complete guide to my life. I opened Lucille's front door, stuffed the condoms into my pocket and led with the cookie plate. We hadn't called Jon and neither had Lucille. I wondered what he was doing home at this time of day.

"Stop dragging your feet. And hold your chin up. You're in charge here. Besides, surprise is on our side," Belle said, slapping open Jon's front door. She strode across the doorstep.

And there stood Lieutenant Jon Stevens in his underwear.

His clothes lay in a heap beside him.

Belle was ahead of me when Jon looked up.

"Jesus. Don't you knock?" Then he realized who was watching him so intently. "Where the hell did you come from?" He looked at Belle.

"Honey?" His voice was low and controlled as his eyes met mine. I was hiding behind Belle.

"Wow, what's that smell?" Belle inched closer to Jon's really nice, mostly naked body. He had just the right amount of everything. Muscle, hair (not much) and other things. They were boxers, so determining his amount of hung-ness was difficult. Which is not to say I didn't try in the few seconds we stared at him.

"Huh? Oh, domestic dispute gone bad. Vomit from the husband, disputed dinner from the wife. Dinner was worse. That's why I'm standing here. ... Shit!" He turned and stomped into the bathroom. I heard the shower running. Five minutes later I heard drawers opening and slamming shut. His problem made me consider, however briefly, my own culinary skills.

"Maybe we should put those clothes in the laundry," I said.

"Maybe we should put them in the garbage." Belle wrinkled her nose.

"Maybe I'll make that decision." Jon was dressed in clean clothes and was rubbing a towel over his damp hair. "Care to tell me about how the two of you got here? And where you've been? Last I knew there was some doubt about where you were and whether you were there voluntarily." He looked pointedly at Belle.

"We drove in a taxi," I said.

"There's a care package for you at Susan Young's condo on Union Street. And by the way, it's Susan Scarpelli." Belle said as if she were handing Jon first prize. She retreated to the kitchen, out of the line of fire.

"Let me guess. The package is wrapped in duct tape. And I know it's Susan Scarpelli. We finally got the connection from Springfield. And speaking of Springfield, what would you like me to tell them?" Jon looked at Belle.

"Nothing. And that package? It's big and ugly and if you don't get it soon, it'll be gone." Belle smiled broadly.

Jon turned back to me.

"You are a constant source of entertainment." He picked up his cell phone. "Yeah, Stevens. Get someone out to attorney Susan Young's condo in the old jail on Union Street. Fast. No, there may be a hostage inside." Jon looked at me again, raising his eyebrows. "I'll meet them over there." I guess the hostage thing bypassed the need for a search warrant.

He pocketed his cell phone, grabbed his gun off the counter, stuffed his shield onto his belt. He was at the door when he turned back. "Stay here. Do not move from this house." And he left. His attitude was beginning to piss me off. Like I couldn't take care of myself. Who had rescued Belle, anyhow?

We lasted 20 minutes. The only real question was where we most wanted to go. Belle wanted to go to Susan's condo. If the goon was still there, she might be able to accidentally stomp on him a few times. Belle had a great deal of confidence in her ability to penetrate police barriers, with some justification. I wanted to go back to Lucille's for more cookies.

We compromised and ate all the cookies we had brought for Jon. Then we got in the taxi and headed toward Susan's condo.

We arrived just as they were bringing the "hostage" out. He looked a little battered, like he'd been rolling around on the floor. His feet had been cut free, but his hands were still taped behind him. He was limping.

Jon came out of the condo after them. When he saw us, the word scowl took on new meaning. He walked over to us.

"What part of stay don't you understand? I feel like I'm training a fucking puppy." He jammed his hands in his pockets. "Ah shit, Susan Young is probably more interested in saving herself than in murdering you. Although if it were up to me, it might be a close call." He looked like he wanted to kick the puppy, but he turned and stomped toward his car instead.

Halfway to the car, he turned around and stomped back to me. He grabbed my face in both hands and kissed me hard on the mouth. Then he walked back to the car, got in and drove away.

"I'll check in tonight, sweetie. Maybe." I smiled and did a little finger wave at the retreating car. Belle stared at the man who was being loaded into a cruiser. I could see visions of trampled flesh running through her brain.

We got in the taxi. The car must have felt the need to be among friends, because five minutes later we found ourselves at the Cool Rides office.

It was late afternoon and all we had eaten was a few dozen cookies, so Mona ordered pizza. Comfort food would help us all talk more freely.

"So," I said, turning to Belle, "what did Susan say to you when they snatched you? What did she want?"

"Mostly she just slapped me around. I think she's into it. Like the S/M thing. Only she was S'n and I wasn't M'n. She'd be real good at the dominatrix trade. She kept screaming about a disc. Said that Horace said to ask me. Bastard. He was always shoving stuff off on me. She ranted about increasing some corridor. I think her daddy has her climbing walls. There's something weird goin' on there. Those Freudian freaks would have a heyday."

"And sometimes a cigar is just a cigar. Maybe she has her own agenda. Have you run this by Jon? I know both of you have a thing about authority, but ..." Mona trailed off. Besides, Jon was pretty busy right now.

"So Horace never kept any books, like about the business? Did he have a computer?" I spoke around a mouthful of cheese and ignored her question. Mona was right about the authority thing, though.

"Not that I knew of."

"Maybe it was his contacts book, on a C.D." Mona said.

"What's a contacts book?" I was new to the language of illicit businesses.

Belle swallowed a bite of cheese, pepperoni, peppers, onions, and something else that I hadn't figured out yet.

"Could be anything from my customers to which police could be bribed. But why would Susan want it? Why wouldn't it be old man Scarpelli who was after it?"

"Or maybe it didn't belong to Horace," I said. "If he got his hands on something like that, where would he hide it? Susan must have searched the apartment before they shot Horace. When you moved in with me, they ransacked my place. Then they staked out Jon's house. Belle, they think you know where some disc thing is."

"I knew Horace inside out. I don't think he had the balls to steal something from Scarpelli. Possibly from Susan, though. He was a sexist pig. He might think a woman wouldn't have the chutzpah to shoot him. Based on my most recent interaction with her, I think she'd enjoy drilling someone between the eyes. She'd like to see brains splatter all over the wall. She'd want to watch someone get hacked up like a pig into pork chops with blood dripping down and pooling on the floor. She'd …" Belle stopped. Mona was staring at her half-eaten piece of pizza. My hand had paused halfway to my mouth. Belle was in her British upper-class mode of speaking, but the words coming out were too coarse for the accent. I wondered if she was aware of how odd it was.

"Okay, we're trying to eat here. Sorry." Belle took another bite.

"Maybe Susan was getting ready to off the old man," Mona said and resumed eating.

This was beginning to read like an episode of The Sopranos. While I was trying to sort out characters, the dispatch phone rang.

"Cool Rides, the best ride ever," Mona purred into the receiver. "Where are you and where do you need to be?" She jotted info on paper. "Short haul. Wal-Mart to Hampshire Heights."

I groaned and looked at Belle. No tip, would probably want us to wait for "just a minute," which would turn into 10 minutes while they dug up the $8, and no wait fee.

"We'll take it," Belle said. She grabbed her bag and headed out the door. I lifted the fare slip from Mona's fingers, shrugged and followed.

When I got into the car, Belle was fastening her seat belt.

"What's with the hurry-up?"

"Hey, we're going to Hamp Heights. I might want to stop at my old digs and pick up a few things."

The fare turned out to be a friend of Belle's from her previous profession.

"Honey, this is Miss Pussy Galore. Named after the wonderful James Bond character with no moral principles whatsoever." Belle waved toward the slightly less spangled but equally voluptuous Pussy. I drove while they reminisced about the good old days of ho.

"I was sorry to hear about Horace. I know how he was, but he did have his good times." Pussy touched Belle's shoulder. "That last day, I remember seeing him skateboarding with the kids. Of course, he stole the skateboard. Maybe that's what got him killed."

"Huh? I don't think those punks would shoot him for swiping their board," Belle said.

Pussy shook her head and gestured with perfectly manicured fingers.

"Oh no. I didn't mean that. He was riding one of the boards. He started getting cocky about how good he was and miscalculated. Rode it straight into the bushes and that board launched Horace right through the front window. It was open 'cause it was hot and the air conditioner wasn't working. It woulda been funny except, well, you know— what happened and all. The next thing I hear a pop. It sure sounded like a gunshot. Musta hit Horace."

"Did you see who did it?" My heartbeat picked up a notch.

She looked at me like I was the dumb duck in the water watching the sharks circle.

"Are you kidding? You hear gunfire around here, you get down. I don't think he knew they were in there. Probably scared the shit outta them when he sailed through the window."

I hadn't asked Jon about the autopsy report. Not that he would have told me anything. I had assumed it was an execution-style shooting. I might pass this information along. If Jon was really nice to me. Or even if he wasn't.

Belle's friend was true to form and emptied the loose change out of her bag to pay the fare. Belle dug a key out and slipped under the police tape, which still hung limply around the crime scene. I collected my money and joined her.

I was on the top step when a wizened old geezer staggered up the sidewalk. His arms were thrown wide, his pants drooped and his fly was open. A little pink penis hung out.

"Belle," he moaned loudly.

Belle stuck her head out the door. "Why, hello, Mr. Ding. What's up?"

Certainly not him, I thought. Mr. Ding stumbled forward.

"For old time's sake?" He wiggled his hips. His penis flopped. He took another step and fell, face first, into the bushes.

"You want me to do something about him?" I asked.

"Is he breathing?"

I leaned a little closer. "Yeah." The air around him smelled horrible.

"Leave him be. He'll sleep it off."

I went inside. "Did you use to … uh … service him?"

"Mr. Ding? God no. I used to cook for him. But he knew what I did. He was forever trying." She smiled.

Never hurts to try. I thought about Belle's previous employment and wondered what it would be like to choose your sexual partners based on their wallets. A lot of women do that. Prostitution was just more upfront about it.

Belle came out of the bedroom stuffing a few spandex tops in her bag. She seemed to have a never-ending supply.

"I've been thinking about where Horace might hide something. I say we search the joint." Belle flipped a cushion off the sofa. There was fingerprint powder on a lot of surfaces. The carpet had an ominous dark brown stain on it.

Belle found mostly dust. All the illegal substances had apparently been confiscated by either the police or, more likely, the murderers.

After 10 minutes, she flopped onto the sofa. The apartment was hot and stuffy. I wandered over to the air conditioner.

"Don't bother," Belle said. "It stopped working three weeks ago. Horace was supposed to get it fixed. He didn't get to it before –"

I punched the power button anyway. The fan came on. It made such a racket I turned it off. "Something's caught in the filter thingy." I gave it a little shake and turned it on again. The rattle got louder. I pulled the filter out. A CD fell to the floor. Well, duh!

I picked it up.

Belle stood up. "Well, what the hell! That's gotta be it."

"Time to go." I had my hand on the door when it flew open, pushing me behind it.

"What the fuck are you doing here?" Susan stepped in and glared at Belle. I kept quiet.

"I fuckin' live here. What are you doing anywhere, bitch?" Belle charged Susan with head down in true dirty wrestling fashion. They toppled down the steps. Belle was on top, so I stayed where I was. Suddenly there was a gun in Susan's hand.

"Back off, bitch!" she screamed. I ducked back behind the door. Belle rolled off Susan and stood up. I retreated behind the counter that separated kitchen from living room.

"Inside." Susan waved the gun at Belle. I grabbed a frying pan off the stove and ducked out of sight.

When I looked out from under the counter, I saw three pairs of feet. One of them was large and masculine. Susan had brought backup. And another pair of nice shoes. Those would be Susan. No matter what else we felt about Susan, she had great taste in shoes. The masculine shoes were big and flat and plain and stood next to the counter. The addition of the bad shoe guy meant not good odds for us. On the upside, neither of them had noticed me.

Chapter 12

"Sit," said Susan, motioning Belle to the nearest chair. Belle sat. Susan stepped forward and slapped her hard across the face.

Belle's arm jerked up defensively and punched Susan solidly in the head. Who doesn't know to tie up their victim first? Stupid. Susan staggered backward, dropping the gun. The bad shoe guy moved forward. I put everything I had into connecting the frying pan with his head and he toppled like a giant sequoia. Susan had the sense to retreat in the face of superior force. She tripped over Mr. Ding on her way out, made it to the car and smoked her tires as she left.

"Bagged another one," said Belle.

I pulled the duct tape out of my purse.

Belle nudged the body with her foot. He didn't move. He was breathing, so we decided to leave him for the police. I added more duct tape. Belle placed a kitchen chair over him and I taped him to that as well. It would make escape a little trickier.

"I need comfort food," I said.

"I want to know what the fuck is on that stupid disc," Belle said.

"And we should call Jon," I added, feeling almost guilty about having found the disc before the cops.

"Lucille will have cookies, and I saw a computer on her desk." said Belle.

Dispatch put me through to Jon. "Stevens." He sounded distracted.

"Hi, Jon." I tried to sound cheery.

"Where are you?" he asked.

"Just leaving Hamp Heights. We had a fare. But you might want to send a squad car over to Belle's old apartment. Where Horace was shot." Where there was crime-scene tape all over the place.

"Why?" Jon's voice was beginning to sound wary, maybe even hostile.

"We left something there for you."

"Does this involve duct tape?"

"Ahhh … yeah."

"Jesus, Honey. Scarpelli might take out a contract on you if this keeps happening." He sounded a bit peevish. "Where are you going now?"

"Belle and I are thinking we might head to your place and stay in tonight."

"How sensible of you. I'll be there as soon as I get the paper done on your latest trophy." He disconnected.

"How's Jon?" Belle smiled one of her you should do it soon smiles.

"He's such a cop. I think he's feeling left out."

"He's just moving in the wrong circles. He hangs with us, he's gonna enjoy life more. Maybe he could enjoy you more, too."

"He's just too controlling. That stuff scares me. He did bust me for no good reason. I was just a kid."

"He busted you? Now that's a story I might need to hear, but yeah, cops do those things. Doesn't mean he can't be good where it counts."

I sighed. It had been a long time since that counted.

"I say let's hit up Lucille and see what she's got cookin'," Bell said.

We rolled Mr. Ding off the sidewalk and hauled him back to his doorway before we left. Belle pushed him back inside his pants and carefully zipped him up.

Of course, Lucille had a batch of cookies in the oven and another on the table.

"Is your computer new?" I asked. My computer skills were nonexistent.

"Oh, my, yes. That's my new baby. I just love the Internet. And all those wonderful ads about penis enlargement. Why, it starts my day off just right. I can show you some of them. I save the best. There's one with a wonderful illustration. It looks a lot like my dearly departed husband. What a shame to cremate that part of him. But they wouldn't remove it for me before they burned him up. I thought about having it preserved." She took a dainty bite of cookie. "So, what do you think about this recipe? Will I get lucky at the senior center tonight?"

I was having trouble getting past the image of jars of preserved penises. "Could you read a disc for us?" I asked.

"Well, of course, dear. I get CDs all the time. They have most of the good classic movies, like Deep Throat, on CD now. I have a very complete collection."

I bet she did. Maybe I could introduce her to Tweedle-dum and Tweedledee.

"Can we, uh, turn this thing on?" asked Belle.

"Boot up Baby? Well of course." Lucille joined her at the computer. She patted it on the side of the monitor and pushed a button. Baby came to life. "Did you want to surf the Net?"

"No, we have a special CD I wanted to take a look at."

Lucille pushed another button. The CD holder slid silently open. I handed her the disc. She set it in the round tray. The holder slid closed. I can identify with computers. You have to push a lot of buttons to get a response.

A list of names flickered onto the screen. Belle crowded in behind me.

"Jesus, I know those names," Belle said. "Some of them work for Scarpelli. And look" – she pointed an enameled nail at a name on the list – "that's a cop." Her perfect finger-nail traced down the list. "Another cop."

It pays to have someone in the business on your side. Belle knew all sorts of people I'd never heard of.

"So, what do you think this is? And why did Susan want it so bad? If it's just Scarpelli's goon squad and some bad cops, that must be pretty common knowledge."

"Susan is relatively new in town. Maybe she wasn't privy to common knowledge," said Belle.

We were contemplating this when there was a knock on the door.

"Should I get my firearm?" Lucille asked.

"No, no firearms. Let me see who it is before we blast them to kingdom come." I stepped to the door and cracked it open.

"Hi, Jon." I opened the door farther.

"Honey." He said it with some wariness in his voice. "You going to let me in?"

"Oh, Jonny, dear. Honey and Belle and I are just having cookies and talking about lists of police officers. Do come in. We have plenty of cookies. And maybe you know some of the officers." Lucille's voice had the maternal ring that she used around Jon.

Jon walked over to the plate of cookies. He took one and continued to the computer. "Playing with Baby again?"

"Did you get my package at Belle's apartment?" I asked.

"Do you know how much paperwork this is taking? We let him go because we didn't have any witnesses who would press charges. You both left and he sure as hell wasn't talking. My fellow officers were taking bets on how you two got him on his back." He eyed me speculatively, then looked at Belle. I turned to the computer.

We stood around Baby with Lucille at the controls. I was having trouble thinking of a piece of plastic and metal as having a name. But then I thought about what things we name. Lots of parts of the human anatomy, for instance. And cars. Willie had names for all the Cool Rides cars.

"Where did you get this?" Jon leaned over. "Shit, what is this? Half of these guys are known felons and the other half are cops. Mostly Springfield cops." Jon scrolled down the list. "Where the fuck did you get this?" He wasn't yelling, really. But his level of frustration at being out of our particular loop was beginning to show.

"Why, Jonny." Lucille patted his hand. "Is this police business?"

Before he had a chance to answer, I jumped in, "I think this is what Susan was after. Horace being killed might have been an accident. Belle's friend heard the shot."

"Wait, wait." Jon needed time to catch up. "We questioned everyone in the Heights. Just who was this witness?" He looked sharply at Belle.

"I ain't talking. She wouldn't be around if there were cops around. Her business ain't compatible with yours. Besides, she didn't see anything. She just heard some shots."

"And she didn't bother to call the police?"

"We talkin' about the same Heights? You hear that sound, you duck and run." Belle's voice dripped scorn. "Duh, reality check."

I could see a tick starting in Jon's jaw. He refocused on the computer screen. "I need to take this CD into evidence."

"How do you know it's evidence of anything you'd be interested in?" Belle was getting belligerent.

"Duh, reality check," Jon replied. His hand moved to pop the CD out of the computer.

Belle slapped his hand away. "Wait a minute. Wait just a damn minute. I remember Horace saying something about some of Scarpelli's men being ready to jump ship. And that the old man was getting a little fuzzy."

"Yeah, I heard that from one of the Springfield cops. They said he was getting ready for the leg breaker in the sky to take him away. They're worried about the aftermath. No heir apparent," said Jon.

"So, maybe Susan was going to move in," I said.

"A woman? Scarpelli would never have approved it. He has a real limited view about what a woman could do. Maybe he just didn't know the right woman." Jon glared at me.

"Yeah, but Susan might not have cared. It wasn't your average father-daughter relationship." Belle was back at the cookie plate. Lucille was staring at the screen.

"I think this is a coup list," Lucille murmured.

"A what?" Jon leaned in closer.

"It's a list of people she could trust. Or people that her father couldn't trust. The cops are dirty. I'm sorry, Jonny, but I think they are." Lucille's face had developed an expression I hadn't seen before.

"If that's what this is, maybe she didn't want Daddy to know about it. He'd recognize it in a heartbeat. If he can recognize anything anymore," I added.

"She'd sure as tootin' kill Horace for it. I wonder which side her husband was taking," Belle said.

"From his status in the morgue, I'd say it was in question, by both sides," said Jon. He reached for the disc.

"Just a damn minute." Belle tried to slap his hand away again. He gave her his cop stare and slowly moved his hand to the disc.

"This is not only evidence. It's dangerous evidence." He removed the disc. "You still don't get it. Two people are dead, possibly because of this list."

Jon turned to me. "And you should have brought this in to headquarters when you found it. You can't just keep evidence until you feel like telling me about it."

"Yeah? And what about Susan being a Scarpelli? When did you plan to tell me about that?" My voice was rising. "If I'd known about that, I might have been more careful when I went to her condo." Knowing that probably wouldn't have stopped me, but I could have slowed down to think about a more rational approach. Jon's attitude was pushing my buttons. I should have been directing my anger toward Susan and her agenda. But Jon was an easy target. I stared at him for 10 seconds and turned and stomped out of Lucille's side of the house, next door and into my bedroom. Which was really Jon's bedroom because it was Jon's house. And that pissed me off even more.

Chapter 13

The next morning, Jon left before I got out of bed. There was a note from Belle telling me she would be at the Cool Rides office. I was feeling stressed and lonely. I decided to see if Lucille would provide the kind of breakfast I was craving. I slung my bag over my shoulder and knocked on her door.

She opened the door. I followed my nose to the breakfast platter.

"Why, hello, dear. Won't you join me?" Lucille said to my back.

I had one cookie in my mouth and another in my hand. Lucille was pouring coffee when we heard a car out in front of the house. We looked out the window.

A long black limo sat ominously at the curb.

"Should I get my gun?" Lucille asked, holding the curtain aside.

As we considered this, a very large man got out of the driver's side. He raised a limp white, lacy square over his head.

"What is he doing?" Lucille moved to the door and opened it a crack.

"Miss Walker?" The driver moved forward cautiously. "Don't shoot. I got Mr. Scarpelli here. He wants to talk. If you could come out to the car."

"Don't let him fool you for a minute." Lucille said. She yelled at the driver, "You tell your boss if he wants to talk to get his ass in here. We women don't get in cars with strangers. Besides, we have cookies."

Whatever her background, Lucille hadn't sprung into life baking cookies. She had a lot of characters in her FBI-jacket-wearing repertoire.

The dark window of the limo glided down silently. A head full of white hair popped out.

"Cookies? Who has cookies?"

"Hey, he's a hot one." Lucille smiled.

"Ah, I think that's Mr. Scarpelli. Should we really let him in?"

"You don't think he would shoot us for chocolate chip cookies, do you? He doesn't look like that kind of man."

"Probably not for the cookies," I admitted. Lots of other possibilities, though.

The driver opened the door and Mr. Scarpelli headed up the walk. Lucille was right. He was stooped and moved slowly but he had piercing dark eyes and Mediterranean good looks. His eyes softened as he approached Lucille.

"Why, what a lovely lady." He took her hand gently in his and raised it to his lips. "And such a heavenly aroma."

"Oh get over it. You can have a cookie. But don't try to charm me into thinking you're just some nice guy. I know who you are. Come on in and we'll negotiate." Lucille turned on her heel and headed for the kitchen. I shrugged and followed.

Mr. Scarpelli had a slight smile on his face. The driver was grinning.

Lucille and Scarpelli sat down at the table. The driver/bodyguard stood behind his boss. I pulled the duct tape out of my bag, set it on the table and took a seat. Mr. Scarpelli kept smiling.

"So, I hear you've met my daughter," he said to me.

It's not usually nice to be ignored. Right now I would have preferred to disappear from the Scarpelli radar.

"Numerous times," I said. With varying results.

Scarpelli devoured a cookie. His bodyguard watched the cookie disappear.

"I got a problem," Scarpelli said. I swallowed hard and had second thoughts about Lucille's gun.

"It isn't you. It's the daughter." He snorted. "Kids – what can you do?" He shook his head in mocking self-defeat.

Shoot her, I thought. Susan Scarpelli Young was a parent's nightmare. Daddy wasn't going to survive his daughter's planned business merger. She was reversing the empty-nest syndrome, watching his nest like a vulture. If it didn't empty, she would empty it. But I didn't really know how he felt about her. Family can be dysfunctional and still have an amazing degree of loyalty.

"Horace – God rest his soul – got something from her, for me. She should take more care with her possessions. I would like to know where this thing is and what's on it. My daughter was quite determined in her pursuit of it. It might help settle some, ah, family differences." Scarpelli stared at me with a tired expression. I reminded myself, again, that he was the ruthless head of a small crime family. If he needed a report to tell him that his daughter was a backstabbing bitch, maybe his level of awareness really was fading.

"My estranged wife may have expressed different opinions about the nature of my business than I would have, to my daughter. In any event, the daughter seems to have a certain view about her place in my life that is not very realistic." He stared off into space and seemed to have lost his train of thought. After a few seconds, his focus drifted back. "She seems to have a somewhat unrealistic view about the whole world, come to think of it. She may be a bit unstable, actually. She doesn't take 'no' for an answer very well." He said this to himself more than to me or Lucille. The bodyguard stared at the floor. "Maybe I shoulda let her run with something. But she don't got the control, and I don't see her learning it either. I don't disapprove of her goals, but her method just ain't gonna work. She's not a real good judge of character." He paused again. "Whatever. I would still appreciate getting back what Horace had."

"Whatever it was, we don't have it." I tried out my own stare. I don't think it worked.

"But you know where it is." Scarpelli's bodyguard moved closer. His looming presence was uncomfortable.

The old man made a gesture and the ape backed up a step. "This thing may reveal some things that are interesting to the wrong people."

Sometimes I'm good at lying, sometimes I'm not. It's lucky I know this. Otherwise some people might get testy.

"It's nowhere you can get it."

"Ah, you gave it to your friend from the police. Well, that won't be a problem for me. A bit inconvenient, perhaps. My daughter will have to get her own ass out of the fire." He turned to Lucille. "Please forgive my language."

Scarpelli rose and was heading for the door when we heard a screech of tires outside. A car door slammed and then Jon's door opened.

Mr. Scarpelli turned when he reached the door. "If you see my daughter, tell her bon voyage for me."

I heard him mumble something as he stood at the door. It sounded like "complete nut-case."

He opened the door and stared straight into Lieutenant Jon Stevens' gun. His bodyguard had one hand full of cookies, and the other one was groping for his own weapon.

"Where is she?" Jon's voice was barely a whisper. He grabbed the old man by the lapels and pressed the gun under his chin. Both Scarpelli and his bodyguard froze. I had never seen that look in Jon's eyes. Hard, cold, scary. Beyond cop face.

"I'm okay. And so is Lucille." I moved to where Jon could see me.

He looked at Scarpelli. "Don't ever come near my house again. Ever." He pulled the old man out the door and released his fist slowly. The bodyguard had seen some secret signal that only those guys know and stopped trying to find his gun. Jon lowered his weapon. I blew out a deep breath that I didn't realize I'd been holding.

"Cookies?" Lucille beamed and pushed the plate across the table. She had turned back into everyone's ditzy grandmother. I felt like I was back from Oz. She slipped the gun back into the kitchen drawer. I hadn't seen it come out.

Scarpelli hobbled slowly to his car, his goon supporting his elbow. Jon stepped into the house, closed the door and sank into the chair recently vacated by Scarpelli.

"What in God's name were you thinking? I can't believe you let him in."

"He wanted me to come out and get in his car. Lucille lured him in with cookies."

"I'm glad you had the brains not to get in a car with him. I think."

"Jonny, he was very sweet," Lucille said.

"Sweet, my ass." Jon frowned. "Are you going to tell me what he wanted?"

"He wanted to know where the disc was. I didn't exactly tell him. He guessed."

"Does he know what's on it?"

"I'm not sure. He seemed to know it implicated his daughter in something, probably illegal. Or maybe just illegal in his system of laws. He views his daughter as a bit unstable."

"Or maybe against his better interests. She might want to watch her back. Probably he should too." Jon stood up.

"I'm going back to work. We haven't finished processing that disc."

"Jon?"

"What?"

"How did you know he was here?"

"I'm a cop," he said. And closed the door behind him.

I considered my morning. I could move back to my now-clean apartment any time. Being there alone with Susan Scarpelli Young still on the loose might not be too smart. But that was only a temporary setback. I had decided to keep the apartment, no matter what either Scarpelli decided to do. Or what Jon decided to do. I needed my space.

Lots of people live with danger. Some people swim in the river with crocodiles. Hell, we all share the universe with millions of asteroids, comets, space dust. You need to be careful when you can. But Susan Scarpelli and her father weren't as inevitable as an asteroid. I resented sharing my space with their danger.

Unfortunately, no matter what anyone else was doing, making rent money was still essential. I had another breakfast cookie, thanked Lucille for her support, and went to work.

Mona had sent Belle out in one of the other cars and was pacing the office, waiting for it to come home.

"She should have been back at least five minutes ago. She's only doing a local."

"If you're worried that someone might try to grab her again, I don't think anyone has her on their agenda right now. They have too many family problems."

"Grab who?" Mona looked at me blankly.

"Belle."

"Who cares about her? If that car comes back with a scratch, I'll have her hide. Or better, I'll have the shoes she was wearing."

"Oh." I fidgeted for a few seconds. "What were they?"

Mona sighed. "Rhinestone high-heeled flip-flops. They would make me at least 4 inches taller."

"Where did she get them? Did you get a source?" Unfortunately, to get the shoes, I had to drive some fares.

I looked at the slip of paper in Mona's hand. "What you got for me?"

Mona smiled and I knew I was going to get one of those fares.

"Wonder Bread man wants a ride home from the grocery store." She grinned. I groaned.

Wonder Bread was introduced in 1921 by the company that makes Twinkies, and you haven't lived until you've had a deep-fried Twinkie. My fare knew his bread history, and anyone who picked him up knew it, too. I heard that before the heat of corporate stress baked his mind, he had been high up in the Wonder Bread company chain. Now he's in city-subsidized housing, but he paid for a cab and if you listened to him, he tipped well. His real name was Tommy.

Tommy stood in front of the mega-grocery with a shopping cart overflowing with blue, yellow and red packages of Wonder Bread. There were a few twinkies tucked in between the loaves of bread. Everything swayed and jiggled precariously, but he made it to the taxi without losing anything and we off-loaded into the backseat. The bottom ones looked squashed, but isn't that part of the appeal?

He wore a black armband and looked morose.

"They're gone!" he wailed. "Gone, gone, all gone."

If he was talking about Wonder Bread, it was because he had just bought the entire supply. I envisioned green mold erupting from his apartment and engulfing Northampton.

"They stopped production. In 10 years, all this bread is going to be worth a fortune to the collectors." Satisfaction mixed with some greed spread across his face like fluffer-nutter on cheap margarine.

He asked me to help move his stash into the elevator and up to his room in the dismal gray cement smudge that is the city's public housing. We loaded up an abandoned shopping cart that sat by the door and headed past senior citizens sitting outside sucking in nicotine. A few followed us in, trailing smoke.

"Hey, is that Wonder Bread? I heard they was closing the plant. Ain't gonna make it no more."

"You're kidding. I was raised on that stuff."

"How come you got so much of it?"

Two more residents hobbled into the group. A few more came out of the restrooms. There were at least 10 wheezing geezers standing around observing the cart over-flowing with plastic sacks of bread.

"You ain't hoarding it, is you?"

The elevator doors opened and I shoved the cart and Tommy inside. As the doors started to close, a wrinkled hand shoved between them and they slid back open. The whole crowd trouped in and the doors shushed together. I was crushed to the back wall.

"I could use a loaf of that for peanut butter and pickle sandwiches. You know it's the only kind of bread that works for that." A gnarled hand reached out and snatched a sack.

"Yeah, I use it for liverwurst with pickles. Them pickles go with everything. And you can get 'em by the gallon at Wal-Mart." Another package disappeared. Two loaves toppled to the floor and were gone.

My fare slapped wildly at grabbing hands.

"Hey, gimme that!" a cracked voice squeaked.

"That one's mine."

"Back off, asshole."

The cart was almost empty when the elevator labored to a stop. The doors creaked open and everyone spilled out into the grungy hallway. I stayed plastered to the back of the elevator. Tommy stood next to me, shoulders slumped in a defeated posture.

I left the cart blocking the door open and peeked into the hall. There were two people still visible. Unless you counted the body on the floor. One of the upright bodies nudged the horizontal one with his toe. The elevator door tried to close, banged the cart and slid back open.

"Don't know where he came from. I heard his head hit the wall. He shoulda known better than to stand in the way like that. Old Ethel there was in a hurry to get home. I wonder if he's dead." He nudged him again.

"I remember when Harry came out into the hall to die."

"Yeah, what a mess he made. Sometimes when you die, you shit in your pants."

"I heard that."

I slipped around the cart and stepped out of the elevator. The door tried to close again, bounced open again.

"So, he's still breathing." One of the old men turned to me.

"I think we should roll him over."

We each pushed with a foot, and the skinny body flopped over onto its back. He looked about 25 years old. He had a number tattoo on his upper arm. It said 18th. I wondered what he was 18th in and why he would be proud enough of coming in 18th to tattoo it on his arm.

"Hey, I recognize him. He was just on the news. You know, one of them bulletins. They said he's wanted for some kind of drug deal. Course, we know that. He had what's-her-face, down the hall, handing out free samples. 'Member that horsey-looking lady, came with him one day? She wanted to swap some funny-looking pills for Anwar's oxystuff. I heard her tell him she was trying out the new territory."

"Yep, he's that drug runner they were trying to catch. He did a high-speed chase, driving a truck full of Porta Potties. Dumped the whole thing on its side and run off into the woods. They never did nab him. Found a bunch of 'suspicious white powder' in the cab of the truck. Porta Potties were clean as a whistle, though. I betcha he's part of some big drug cartel. Think there's any reward?"

The other old guy whipped open his cell phone and dialed 911. He turned to me. "You know this ain't just any old subsidized housing. We're a regular stop on the interstate drug-running corridor. I read that in one a them national magazines."

Any drug runners who stopped in here were putting their lives in danger. Unless they were supplying the senior citizens who lived here, their chances of survival were pretty poor. I wondered what kind of samples were being passed out. The apartment complex housed a population of elderly and disabled, many of whom were on a variety of medications. I could see some enterprising business springing up around the heavier painkillers.

The body groaned.

"Maybe we should tie him up." The old guy pulled a roll of duct tape out of his baggy pants.

My fare finally staggered out of the elevator and looked sadly at the last three loaves of bread in the shopping cart.

"It's nice to know they like the stuff so much," I said, trying to put a positive spin on it. He shuffled out and down the hallway, dragging the cart behind him. The elevator doors finally closed. I took the stairs.

The police cars were pulling up when I got to the lobby. Jon's unmarked was first in line.

"How's your duct-tape supply?" he asked.

"Are they sending detectives to bust senior citizens now?" I snapped back.

"Dispatch said we should look for a Cool Rides cab. I thought it might be you."

"It was all about Wonder Bread," I said.

Jon shook his head. He looked at me and smiled. He leaned over and handed me a stray loaf that must have fallen out of the cab.

"I can't keep up with your crime-fighting spree." He looked toward the building.

"So where's the body?"

"Upstairs, third floor. And he's alive."

"Contained?"

"Very."

"Duct tape?"

"Yes, but it's not mine," I said defensively. "It was the senior-citizen brigade."

Jon motioned to the uniforms and they went inside. "Any idea who it is? Or why 911 called us?"

"Those old people watch news television 24/7. They saw the guy on one of the local channels, a trucker who fled the scene after a high-speed on the interstate. Something about Porta Potties and suspicious powder and being a stop on the drug runners' route. He has a tat that says he's 18th in something."

"Shit, 18th Streeters, Porta Potties and white powder. That just makes my day," he said, looking a little over-whelmed. "I need to talk to that guy and maybe some of those senior citizens. And I'll talk to you later," he said and disappeared inside.

Jon knew things he wasn't telling me. In a small com-munity, people share stuff with a taxi driver. Jon wasn't sharing.

So, I live in the moment. Tommy had paid up before the riot. I got a loaf of sort-of bread out of it. Thinking about the guy at the city housing and drug runners, I headed back to scare up more rent money. Crime in Northampton is either personal and domestic-related or drug- and money-laundering-related. The domestic problems are local. The drug and money laundering are controlled from outside the city. The victim of the Wonder Bread riot was an outsider. It got me thinking about how important Northampton was to the drug trade. I remembered the two guys who had approached me about buying the cab company and wondered again about Northampton and its criminal activities. Were they criminals looking for something? What?

Not my job to know. But I felt like I was getting sucked into something I wasn't comfortable with.

Lunch was on the table when I got to Cool Rides. It was pizza loaded with everything except, thank God, Wonder Bread.

"So how was he?" Mona asked around a mouthful of sausage.

"We had a little accident."

Mona rushed to the window to check out the car.

"Not the car. The car is fine. No scratches, no dents. Honest." I told them about the bread riot.

"Yeah," Belle said, "those old folks, they have real chutzpah. Gotta be careful around them. Look at Lucille. She's murder with those cookies."

A pretty good shot with a large gun, too.

"I don't think it was the senior citizens fighting over bread that brought the cops." I turned to Mona. "You got anything for me?"

"Yeah, King Street porn store to Easthampton. Don't worry," she said at my look of dismay. "It's one of the clerks."

"Like he's gonna be normal." I turned back to Belle. "Want to come along? You still need some drive-time experience."

"Yeah, from superpro driver here." Belle got up and headed for the door. "I can run bodyguard. Protect you from the big bad porno clerk."

I rolled my eyes and followed her out.

We picked him up and delivered him to an apartment building in Easthampton. Belle fidgeted the whole way, bouncing her leg, cracking her knuckles, shifting in her seat. He paid up and disappeared into the shabby building. He was big and mean-looking. I tried to envision him selling accessories to horny senior citizens.

"Excuse me sir, but how many tubes of lube did you want with that elephant-sized dildo?"

When he was out of sight, I turned to Belle. "Okay, what is wrong with you? You're acting like there's a bomb in your britches."

I backed into a side street to turn around.

"I know that guy. I saw his portrait in the police station. He's up for a mob hit."

"Are you sure? Some of those wanted pictures are pretty fuzzy. And way out of date."

"I know who he is," Belle said with certainty.

I studied the side-by-side brick buildings where we dropped him. There was a narrow alley between them that dead-ended into a brick wall. Unless you like brick, the landlord wasn't charging for the view. The side door emptied into the alley.

Suddenly the door slammed open. A woman charged out, with our fare in hot pursuit. He grabbed her hair with one hand. The other hand was holding a gun. The woman lost the battle to get away. He forced her to her knees, raised the gun and pressed it to her head.

I jammed the car into drive and mashed the accelerator to the floor. We squealed out of the side street and careened into the alley. The guy's head jerked up. He dropped the woman. She did a fast crawl back to the doorway. He turned toward the cab. Too late, asshole. He must have thought the same thing, because he wheeled around, took two steps, smacked into the brick wall, bounced off and planted his butt on the hood of my car. I slammed on the brakes. When I opened my eyes, he was spread across the front of the car. His hand twitched, and he slid to the ground.

Belle called 911. I got out of the car to find the gun. His victim had come out of the doorway and was looking for it, too. I found it first, probably because she had stopped to kick him a few times. I was less inclined to shoot him than she might have been.

By the time the cops arrived, the guy was starting to come around. They checked his pulse, cuffed him and loaded him into the back of the cruiser. His lady friend and one of the cops disappeared into the building. Jon had been visiting the Easthampton station, swapping paperwork, when the call came in. He stood with Belle and me while the Easthampton cops did their thing. The other cop came over to Jon.

"You know who that guy is?" He glanced at me. "That's Ruzzi. He's wanted in five states for murder. They finally got enough evidence to nail his ass in New Jersey."

"Jesus, Ruzzi. Did you get all his weapons?" asked Jon

"Two guns, a knife and a bottle of something." The other cop looked at me again.

"Strip-search him when you get to the station. Mean-time, keep your gun handy. What the hell is he doing here? He's a freakin' mob hit man. Shit." Jon looked like he wanted to kick something. The name Scarpelli wandered around in the back of my head.

"You want to take him to Northampton?" the cop said, pride of possession battling with the reality of a truly bad guy.

"Nope, he's your collar. Just be careful. I'll do inter-views with the taxi driver for you." Jon turned back to me.

"Honey, you are truly frightening," he said and left.

Belle and I went back to Cool Rides. When you're high on adrenaline, it's best to keep moving. Belle went to a pickup at the movie theater. Mona handed me a slip.

"This one is an accident. No fatalities. No serious inju-ries. Just need a ride back to town."

"Who called it in?"

"Lieutenant Jon was on his way back from Easthampton when a car crashed coming the other direction. He called the ambulance, the tow truck and us. Said something about you being a scary woman. What's that about?"

"I don't know. I just do my job. Bye."

Jon was still at the scene when I pulled up. The loving couple had declined medical treatment, so the EMTs declared everyone very lucky and left. The tow truck was leaving with a bent-in-half car. A tree on the side of the road had lost some skin.

"Hey, hi again," I said to Jon.

"Hi yourself. I wondered if Mona would send you."

"So what happened? Talking on the phone?"

"Nope." Jon grinned. "The driver's airbag deployed."

"Before or after the crash?"

"His fly was unzipped. And her face had a lot of airbag burn."

Too much information. "Can I safely put them in my cab? How indecent are they?"

"I doubt they'll be using that part of his anatomy for a while. She locked her jaw when they crashed." Jon leaned against the tree with his legs crossed.

I dropped the couple from hell in downtown Northampton. He said she was an insatiable nymphomaniac. She said he was a manipulating cocksucker and from now on he could suck his own cock, 'cause she sure as shit wasn't going to. They split the fare and argued over that. They didn't split the tip, because there wasn't one.

I headed back to the office. The phone rang as I walked through the door. Belle had returned and volunteered to ride along.

"Yeah, we could do that." Mona flipped the phone closed. "Woman wants a ride out to the bridge as soon as possible. Pick up in front of the Hole bar."

The Coolidge Bridge is named after President "Silent Cal" Coolidge. It's the only way to cross the Connecticut River from Northampton unless you want to go 20 miles north to the next bridge or find out if your car floats. A lot of people go north because the bridge out of Northampton has been under construction since maybe Silent Cal's time. There's always too much traffic and it's always backed up, inducing occasional cases of bridge rage.

We picked the fare up in front of the bar. She carried a huge shoulder bag and listed a bit to that side and settled heavily into the backseat. She didn't look old enough to be drinking.

"So," Belle said. "You going out to the bridge for a swim?"

"I'm going to jump off and kill myself." She opened her bag and took out a medium-sized brick.

"You have got to be shittin' me." Belle turned in her seat to get a better look at the woman and the brick. "Lady, no one takes a cab to commit suicide. You better pay me right now. And a big tip would be nice. So we don't take a detour to the police station. And that brick – that ain't gonna do a thing. You want us to stop at the hardware store first and get you a cement block? I mean, how serious are you about this? 'Cause if you change your mind, we charge a wait fee."

A cabbie's first concern is collecting payment, but I thought Belle was being a bit insensitive. I turned around. "Fasten your seat belt, please. You can kill yourself, but if I kill you, it's going to raise my insurance rates."

Belle and I stared at her. She fastened the belt.

173

"Okay? Happy?" She did the teenage pout and slouch.

Oh, yeah.

"So, what you want us to do? About that silly little brick. I mean, you need to get realistic about this. The fall will probably kill you, but just in case, we should get a cement block, and some rope would be good, too. And, hey, are you old enough to commit suicide without your parents' permission?" Belle gave the woman the raised-eyebrows look.

"I'm 17 years old. And my mother doesn't care what I do." More pouting. "You really think the fall will kill me?"

"Sweetie, it's over a hundred feet before you hit the water. That's like hitting a sidewalk from a 10-story building. You're gonna be a mess. But most likely you'll be too dead to worry about how you look. Of course, you could have dressed better." Belle gave the girl's outfit the once-over. It was blah and baggy.

"You got clean underwear on?" I asked. "'Cause in my limited experience with suicide, clean underwear would be high on my list of stuff to do before."

The young woman's bottom lip quivered a little. We reached the parking lot next to the bridge. "I don't need a bigger brick. I got three of them in here. I'm going to hang the pocketbook around my neck."

"Oh, that'll look real nice. It'll probably fly up and smack you in the nose on the way down. I hope you didn't ask for an open casket, 'cause your nose will be flat, flat, flat. You did make some arrangements for after?" Belle opened her door and got out.

"I didn't really think about all that. Suicide seemed like the simple way out. I guess it's more complicated than I thought." Our passenger had begun to look more morose and less certain. Belle held the door open.

"Well, come on then. Honey and I will walk up with you. We can throw one of the bricks off. That way, you can test the distance. See how long it's going to take you to hit."

"Why do I need to know that?"

"You want your last minutes on earth to be quality time, don't you? It's good to know how many you got. That way you can do something worthwhile with them." Belle started to walk up the sidewalk that crosses the bridge. She turned back to our young passenger. "That's $8, by the way."

The girl looked at her blankly. "The fare, sweetie. It's eight bucks."

"Oh, yeah." She started digging in her bag. She came up with two dollar bills and a lot of quarters.

I sighed. "Keep the change. It'll help weigh you down." I got out of the car.

We all went about a third of the way up the bridge. Belle and I were walking faster than the girl who was slowed down by her load of bricks. We stopped to let her catch up. Belle leaned over the railing. "This is probably far enough. Should do the trick." We were over the water now. I knew that no one had ever died jumping off this bridge. Our young passenger must not have had that piece of information.

She caught up with us and stared over the railing.

"What's your name anyway? You know, for when the cops ask us if we knew you. That's if they find your lily-white, crushed and broken, bloody, chewed-on-by-fishes body. Be good to have a name. And any special reason for doing this thing, just in case the press wants a caption for that photo on the front page."

"Umm, my name's Galaxy."

"Galaxy?"

"What?"

"No, I mean that's your name?"

"Yeah, why?"

"It's a real interesting name."

"My mom's an astrologer."

"Your mom, huh. So give me one of those bricks." Belle held out her hand.

"I guess two will be enough." Galaxy reluctantly slipped a brick into Belle's hand. "My mom told me I couldn't go to the hospital to visit my friend. She overdosed on heroine. She's only 15. She doesn't have very many friends. She has some problems with drugs and all that shit, but she's really a good person."

"Your mom?"

"My friend!" Galaxy rolled her eyes. "Mom said she was a bad influence and she didn't want me around friends like that."

"Oh." Belle hefted the brick in her hand. "So, let's see how this goes down. Honey, you got a watch with a second hand?"

I raised my hand. "One, two, three." Belle dropped the brick.

"Bombs away." We all watched it careen toward the water. It dropped like a, well, a brick. Splat.

Galaxy stood back from the railing.

"How long?" Belle asked.

"Less than 30 seconds." A lot less, but I didn't want her to think it would be over quickly, so I didn't say that it only took about five seconds for the brick to go from being a weight in Belle's hand to being a ripple in the water. Galaxy's eyes had followed the brick from Belle's hand and were now glued to the ripple.

"Wow, I could have an orgasm in 30 seconds." Belle smiled.

I looked at her.

"Well, if I really concentrate," she said.

Galaxy shifted her gaze to her feet. "So how much will it cost to take me back to town?" she murmured in a small voice.

"Sweetie, why don't we take you home?" I put my hand on her shoulder. "No charge." Sucker, I thought to myself.

We all trooped back off the bridge, loaded up and took her home.

Her mother was so grateful to see her that we watched the hugs and tears for a few seconds.

"I'm so sorry I said those things about your friends. Friends are important."

"I'm sorry I said you would never see me again."

Then Mom noticed us. "Who are you? And where did you find her?"

"Cool Rides Taxi, ma'am." I handed her a card.

"Mom, I think I owe them some money."

"Oh, let me get my purse." Mom dug around and handed me a 50-dollar bill. "Keep it. I can't tell you how grateful I am."

We left them at the kitchen table with sodas and chips. The junk-food equivalent of cookies and milk. I thought about mob hit men, drug runners, and all the horrible stuff Jon had to face in his job. Even if her friend had somehow landed in the hospital, this young girl lived in a nice house in a nice neighborhood in a nice town. I thought of the kids from Holyoke and Springfield growing up with drive-by shootings, surrounded by drugs. Suicide seemed like an overreaction. But she was a teenager.

"Wow, that wiped me out. I need fuel." Belle settled into the cab.

I called Mona. "Cool Rides Cab, where are you and where do you need to be?" she sang into the phone. "Oh yeah, you guys. You can head home. Night shift is here."

We headed to Jon's house. He greeted us at the door.

"Been a full day on the crime-fighting front?" I asked.

"For both of us, as I recall."

"Yeah, we've been busy saving lives," Belle said. "And busting heads. I'm calling takeout." Belle thumbed through a stack of menus by the phone.

"Let's see … we got Chinese, we got more Chinese, and more Chinese. Ah, here we got Italian, and Indian, and Mexican, and pizza … and Chinese.

"Lucille brought us cake. Should go well with Chinese."

Jon pointed at the counter. "And she left a package for you." He handed me a manila envelope.

I pulled scissors out of some deep recess in my bag and sliced it open. Jon was looking over my shoulder as I stared at the multicolored, Day-Glo, extra-sensitive, extra-large condoms. The note said, "Hope you get to try these out. I'm still waiting to get lucky. Let me know if I should invest in a box for myself. Enjoy, Lucille."

I blushed and slapped the envelope closed. Jon's fingers rested on my neck. I whipped around and took a step backward. He grinned.

"Love Lucille, she's always looking out for my best interests."

"Are you laughing at me?"

"Absolutely." Jon looked at the envelope. "And with you."

"You aren't laughing with me. I'm not laughing. I'm not even smiling."

"I could change that. I could make you smile all night and half of tomorrow."

Self-confident bastard. But he was probably right. Of course, he would be smiling, too.

I was edging forward when the doorbell rang. Belle came out of the bedroom.

"Give the man some money," she said, snatching the bags and heading for the kitchen.

An hour later, we slowed to a nibble and the rest went into the fridge for breakfast.

Belle had another choir practice. That meant a severe dress-down. Her boob-announcing spandex top became a plain white shirt. Her butt-enhancing pants changed into a long black skirt.

Jon looked at her appraisingly. "Changed our wicked ways?"

"Mine were never wicked. But I bet yours haven't changed one bit. Don't wait up, sweeties." She sashayed out the door.

Jon started clearing the dishes. I put my plate in the dishwasher. I turned for the next plate and ran into Jon's chest. I stood there, staring at his shirt. I put a tentative hand on his chest.

Suddenly, we were kissing and stumbling toward his bedroom. We were through the door and on the bed. His hand was under my shirt and heading upward when I heard a distant ringing.

Jon yanked the offending phone off his belt and tossed it over his shoulder. It hit the wall with a thud, dropped to the floor and stopped ringing. His lips were working their way down my neck and his hand was working its way up my body when the land line started ringing. His hand slowed and his mouth stopped.

"Shit." He rolled away. "I have to get that. Probably work."

Telephonus interruptus. He seized the phone.

"What?" he snapped. "And this better be good." He listened for a few seconds. "You have got to be kidding. And you need me because?" He listened for a few more seconds.

"Rank?" he yelled into the phone. "Bust me to foot patrol for the night, for Christ's sake. Yeah, okay."

Jon flopped back onto the bed. "I have to go in. They're about to do a takedown and they need my Lieutenant-hood."

"What happened?"

"Two idiots tried to pull the front off an ATM."

"And they didn't catch them?"

"They took off after the ATM pulled the bumper off the truck. They left the bumper attached to the ATM."

I grinned. "With the license plate still attached."

"Yep. DMV says they live off King Street. I'll be back. Don't move."

My body was pulsing like a bass drum and he thought I would stay there for the hours it took them to grab the bad guys, process them and finish the questioning? I needed a cold shower or a long walk. I thought about walking to Belle's choir practice. But that was probably a no-no in Jon's book. Having the Scarpelli gang interested in my whereabouts was getting creepy. I took the shower.

Jon wasn't home when I fell asleep and I didn't find him in my bed in the morning, so either he had gone into work early or not come home at all.

Chapter 14

When I got up the next morning, the house was empty. I stopped at the drive-through and arrived at work with jelly doughnuts for Mona, hoping they would get me some airport fares.

When I walked in, Mona snatched the box and replaced it with a fare slip.

"Mr. Pettibone needs a ride to the bank out on King Street, near the construction site." An aging mini-mall was being rebuilt. The only thing left upright was a branch of the local bank.

Mr. Pettibone lived on Fruit Street, at the edge of the commercial district. I waited at the door while he tucked a blanket around his elderly wife.

"I'll be back real soon. I'll make it better, I promise." He kissed her cheek and followed me out. His hands were shaking as he pulled the hood of his sweatshirt over wispy white hair. The open-ended pocket on the sweatshirt bulged, giving him a potbelly. His eyes were clouded with age. His shirttail hung out and one shoe was untied.

"You want me to take you up to the Main Street bank? I can wait while you go in. Be quicker than going all the way to King."

"I got a friend out at the King Street branch," he mumbled, keeping his head down. "I gotta get some money to buy some medicine."

"Okay," I said. I eased up the hill through downtown. Traffic was heavy, the sidewalk teemed with pedestrians, and jaywalkers were rampant, each doing a self-righteous dance between the cars trying to negotiate downtown. Mr. Pettibone twitched in his seat.

"Can't you, like, take a shortcut or something? If I were driving, I'd know a shortcut. And I'd be going faster. And I'd use the horn a lot. Maybe I should be a taxi driver."

And thank God you're not, I thought. I liked Mr. P, but he seemed really stressed today.

"I need to do the bank thing, and then I need to go to the drugstore and get some medicine for my wife. I got the prescription right here." He pulled a piece of paper out of the pocket of his sweatshirt.

I stopped at a traffic light and looked at Mr. P. There was a tuft of blond hair sticking out of his pocket.

"Maybe you could let me off at the bank and wait around the corner." His hands were shaky and in constant motion.

That sounded ominous. He stuffed the prescription back into the sweatshirt pocket and a gun bounced out the other end onto the floor. He moved his foot over on top of it. And squashed it flat.

"Mr. P., what is going on?" I pulled around the corner and over to the side of the street.

"I told you, I gotta get some money for my wife's medicine."

"Do you have an account at the bank?"

He leaned over and picked up the plastic gun. He tried to bend it back into shape. "Not really," he said. "But this medicine costs more than our rent. We never needed this stuff before."

"Don't you think someone at the bank might recognize you?"

"I got this." He pulled out a rubber Joan Rivers mask.

"Mr. Pettibone, you have trouble remembering to tie your shoes. You really think you can rob a bank with a flat plastic gun?"

"They'll never think an old geezer like me would do it. Can you wait around the corner while I do the job? I could do it once a month. Then we could afford that stuff."

"You don't have any health insurance, do you?"

"I got some insurance. Life. Took it out so my missus wouldn't hafta pay for my bein' put in the ground."

"Health insurance, Mr. P. Who pays for your doctor's visits?"

"Never went to the doctor before. The Missus had to go up to the hospital. They were real nice. Fixed the missus up with some medicine and told me to go get more. I tried to pay them, but they just kept handing me papers. Finally I gave up and left."

Bank robbery isn't exactly a stable profession, but maybe better than Social Security or Medicare. A lot less paperwork. And then I thought about the real guns that the police, who would probably want to stop a bank robbery, had. And the gun that had killed Horace. Mr. Pettibone needed to dump the gun before he got shot and get health insurance, in case he got shot. I pulled into traffic and hung a left.

"Hey, this ain't the way to the bank."

"I'm taking you to get free medicine." I didn't know how to make the intricacies of the modern medical system clear to Mr. Pettibone, but I did know where to get him freebies. And I knew that the people at the drop-in center would get his paperwork done.

I parked in front of the old Masonic building that houses the emergency shelter in Northampton and, during off hours, the drop-in center. A lot of interesting people hang out there, and that feeling of being watched crept up my back. I didn't think it was related to Susan Scarpelli. Some people specialize in watching. I pulled Mr. P out of the cab, shoved the plastic gun under the seat and we shuffled into the drop-in office.

"Meds," I said to the woman sitting next to the desk. "He has the script. He needs a note for the pharmacy."

She pulled out forms and started filling them in. She turned to me. "You need transport money?"

"Can you pay me, Mr. P?"

He looked at his untied shoes. The woman made out a check to Cool Rides. She turned to Mr. P.

"Take this to the downtown pharmacy. They'll charge it to us. This is a one-month supply. Come back here in

a week and I'll have your medical card ready. Sign here."
She pushed the paper over for his signature and handed me
the check. It included a tip. God, I love this town.

After the pharmacy stop, I took Mr. P home. By the end
of the week, he would know more about the services available to people in need than the governor, the mayor and
any of the politicians who had passed legislation creating
the services combined. The volunteers at the drop-in center
knew the ropes.

Northampton takes care of its people in need. The
problem with a vulnerable population is that it attracts
predators. The Scarpelli family provides the predators.
How that predation could be kept under control was the
problem that Jon and the rest of the Northampton police
had to deal with daily. I remembered the senior citizens
talking about the drug trade in their apartment building.
Mr. P. and his wife had survived on their own for a lifetime.
They hadn't needed medical assistance or even housing assistance before. And that made me think about my trashed
apartment and that made me think about Susan Scarpelli
and that made me remember that she was still on the loose.

I wondered if she was the one who had trashed my
place. Old man Scarpelli was after the same disc. He might
have searched, but he wouldn't have trashed the place. I
might not even have known he'd been there. Whoever
did it probably wore gloves, if only to avoid getting the
mess on their hands. I lived in the Grand Central Station of
fingerprints anyway. Belle's and my fingerprints would be
the first ones to pop out of the system. Mine because Jon
had busted me once, long ago and far away. Belle claimed
she had never been busted. Did they print witnesses? Did
I believe her?

I swung back by Cool Rides to see what Mona might have for me. If shoe shopping was on the agenda for later, I would have to get a few more fares.

Before I got out of the car, Mona had a fare slip in my hand. I spent the day running kids to doctors' appointments and soccer practice, people loaded with electronics and oversize televisions from Wal-Mart to subsidized housing, mumbling dental patients, temporarily blind eye patients and impatient college students who had forgotten that the buses don't always run on time. Mona called on my way back from a junk-food run for a local stoner.

"Annie needs to go to the liquor store. You're up." That was fine. I could get some beer to stock my apartment fridge while Annie got her sherry.

I picked her up at the retirement home. Her cocktail hour is notorious. Old-lady sherry is strong stuff.

"Now, mind you," said Annie as she got in the cab, "I never drink before 5 o'clock. What time is it now? And I never drink all day Monday. Just to make sure I can go a whole day without. What day is it today? Is it 5 o'clock yet?"

"It's almost 4 o'clock and it's Tuesday. We'll have you home in time for cocktails." I parked in front of the liquor store and trailed in behind her. I headed to the beer aisle. She grabbed an extra-large shopping cart and forged her way to the sherry.

The beer aisle in a big liquor store overwhelms me with the wonderful and exotic. I end up with Budweiser. It's mostly for guests anyway. If they want exotic, they can BYOB.

I was staring at beer when I heard Annie's shrill and angry voice. Her eyesight is terrible and her hearing is worse. Sometimes she thinks the clerk cheats on the change.

"And don't you ever butt ahead of me in line again, young man."

When I got to the counter, Annie was holding a monster sherry bottle by the neck. The clerk had his hands in the air and his mouth open. There was a body on the floor. Then I noticed the gun. I leaned over and pried it out of the body's hand. I laid it carefully on the counter. It wasn't plastic. The clerk lowered his hands and leaned over to see the body better.

"Golly, lady. Thanks."

"Well, I never. He was about to cut the queue. No one butts in front of me. I don't care what he needed. I had my sherry all set and he had no right."

I sighed and pulled out the duct tape. It had been a boring afternoon. I guess I was due for a duct-tape experience.

"Did you hit the alarm?" I asked the clerk.

"No, but jeez. The boss is going to be rip shit. We get charged for the alarm. Maybe I could just call the police business line." He looked at Annie and me for approval.

"Well, I don't think you need police for cutting the line. But whatever you think is best. Could we go now? Is it 5 o'clock yet?" Annie asked.

"It's always 5 o'clock somewhere, but we need to wait here a few more minutes."

I told the clerk to hold off while I speed-dialed Jon's cell phone and explained the situation. I held it away from my ear while he ranted about civilian involvement.

"Are we fighting?" I asked.

"No, I'm not close enough to fight. But I will be in five minutes. Will it make a difference if I say don't move?"

I clicked the phone closed.

Annie said, "Just as long as we get home by 5 o'clock. What day is it? Is it Monday? I certainly hope not. I could really use a drink."

"It's getting closer to 5." And by the time she got back, it would be close enough.

Jon arrived and took a look at the guy in tape. "Shit, that's Lenny Zipco."

"You know him?"

"He's a small-time heroin dealer out of Springfield. The supply lines must be in really bad shape if the dealers are holding up liquor stores."

"Maybe dealing heroin isn't scary enough for him," I said, thinking about supply lines. What kind of supply lines did they have that were in such bad shape? I, again, recalled the Godfather guys who had offered me help in buying the taxi company in exchange for some kind of undefined favors.

"Probably safer," Jon answered.

They finished loading the groggy would-be robber into the patrol car, getting a statement from Annie that mostly addressed the bad manners of this younger generation, the clerk who commented on the sturdiness of the sherry bottle, and me, who had arrived after the fact. It was 4:30. Annie could have her drink as soon as she hit the retirement home.

Jon stared at me, eyes narrowed, scowling in frustration.

"What part of don't move don't you understand?"

"I figured you'd be home late."

"Tonight, I'm going to cuff you to the bed."

Hmmmm.

Maybe tonight would be a good time to move back to my apartment. I dropped Annie off at her condo in the retirement village. She offered me a nightcap. It was nowhere near night, but respectable enough for cocktail hour. I declined and headed back to Cool Rides.

Mona, Willie and Belle were playing cards when I trotted through the door. There was a stack of driver applications sitting on the table next to Mona. They looked untouched. We currently had four drivers if you counted Belle and Willie. We had five cars.

"Spit!" Willie laid down his cards with a grin. It looked like Belle had made the grade as a driver.

"So, how was your day?" I asked her.

"I think there's something in the air today," she grumbled.

"Yeah? What happened?"

"The first fare was a mother and daughter fighting over cleaning guess whose room. Then a father and son arguing about school. Then a couple fighting over sex. She's screaming, he's yelling. All of a sudden, they start groping like friggin' porn stars. It's getting so hot I have to up the air conditioning. I made it to the house just before the zippers came down. He throws a 50 at me and they jump out like their pants are on fire. It was a 10-dollar fare."

"Are we going shoe shopping?"

For a minute, I thought Belle was blushing. With her color, it was hard to tell.

"Nah. After I dropped them off, I swung by the porn store and blew the tip on a new vibrator.

"I took a break after the next three fares in a row propositioned me. I need to go clothes shopping. Taxi driving and ho work need different duds."

"Maybe you need to cut the bling a little," I said. Her glittering spandex top caught sunlight coming in the window. I squinted at the blinding sparkle bouncing off her barely contained chest. "And maybe a higher neckline?"

I looked down at my plain T-shirt, faded jeans and worn sneakers. There had to be a middle ground that would de-bling Belle and re-bling me.

She picked up a few cards and laid them on the table. "See, I might have got you in the next hand," she said to Willie.

The landline started ringing. Mona picked it up.

"Honey, it's for you. The lieutenant, I think."

Belle waved at the phone. "Say hi for me."

I stepped into the office and closed the door.

"Hi, what's up?"

"I'm coming over to pick you and Belle up and take you to my house. I'll be there in 10 minutes. Don't move! I mean it, Honey."

"Wait," I squeaked. "I need to take a cab home with me tonight. I'm scheduled to work at 9 tomorrow. What's so important?"

"We'll talk when I get there." Click. I hate being hung up on.

Chapter 15

"What's Mr. Yumm say?" Belle was laying out a game of solitaire.

"He's more than a cute butt. And he'll be here in five minutes."

"And?"

"And we'll talk." I shrugged.

Jon pulled up in front of the garage and came in.

"Honey, Belle." Jon nodded to us. "We need to talk."

"Uh-oh, he's got his cop face on. I really don't like that one." Belle said and moved a few cards around. Me either. It usually means there's going to be a control issue.

"We found your friend Bozo, whose name, by the way, was Lester Cardozzo."

"Was?" I had a bad feeling suddenly.

"He bailed out yesterday and was head down, feet up at a construction site in Springfield by morning. He was in the

Porta Potti, shot in the back of the head, which was in the hole, so to speak. The other two have declined bail."

My stomach did a fast roll. I didn't like Bozo. He had put a gun in my face, kidnapped Belle and, I had no doubt, done some very nasty things. Not a nice person. But he had become a passing acquaintance, and I didn't know many people who had died violently and died young. He wasn't much older than me. Some mother, somewhere, would grieve, maybe. I grabbed the table and pushed my chair back. Belle glanced up at my face, turned over the ace of spades with one hand and casually reached over and pushed my head down between my legs with the other.

Jon came around the table and put a hand on my back. "Breathe deep," he said. "So, I'm thinking either Scarpelli is cleaning house or Susan Young is in panic mode. The Springfield police are watching Scarpelli. A body in their jurisdiction convinced them to cooperate in the investigation." He paused.

"His daughter is another question. We can't find her. You two will stay at my place until we do. She may be operating on her own. Right now she's a person of interest in enough murders to bring her in for some questions." Jon rubbed my back. None of this was a request. My defiant personality tapped me on one shoulder and whispered, "Make your own decisions." My manipulating side tapped the other shoulder and said, "You can use this situation!" Somewhere between my shoulder blades, caution raised its ugly head. There wasn't any room left for normal.

I straightened up slowly. "I'm okay now. Yeah, we could keep the sleepover thing going a while longer." I looked at Belle.

"Hey, having our own house cop around right now might be just dandy."

Jon narrowed his eyes at her and grunted. I doubted he meant to stay home and guard us. He was in hot-pursuit mode.

Although my job required some independence, I knew when to pick my fights. Jon had to go to work tomorrow morning, too. I was pretty sure he wasn't going to handcuff me to the bed. Even if he did, Belle was on my side, and between the two of us, we could defeat any restraints Jon had.

We trooped out to Jon's car. He got into the driver's side. I looked wistfully at my taxi. Tomorrow was soon enough. Jon's house was an easy walk to the garage. Mona needed drivers as much as drivers needed her. I was pretty sure she would give me some fares. If Belle and I stuck together and stayed alert, we'd probably be safe enough. At least from Susan Scarpelli. The rest of the crazies out there were another problem.

We spent the evening eating more takeout Chinese and watching the comedy channel. I temporarily forgot my problems in the face of Stephen Colbert's brain-candy comedy. Jon went back to work for a few hours and didn't get home until I was in bed and asleep. He left before I got up. Unless he had the time to check up on us, Belle and I were on our way uptown. We could snag coffee and a taxi. Nutrition plus rent.

It was a glorious summer day, not a cloud in the sky, yada, yada. The walk was nice. We loaded up on caffeine and sugar and headed down to Cool Rides.

Mona looked suspicious, but she handed me car keys and two slips. Both were local short hauls. They wouldn't pay much rent, but they might help Belle get a more appropriate wardrobe.

The first pickup was Valerie Crumrine. She wanted a two-block ride from State Street to the dance studio on King Street. In the taxi business, you're selling transportation. Telling your customers to get their ass in gear and walk just isn't done.

Valerie hurled her 5-foot-5-inch, 200-pound body down the three concrete steps. She landed in a heap on the grass next to the taxi. She rolled over and stood up.

"I'm fine. I do that a lot. I'll be good, great." She bent to get in the car and slammed her head into the door.

"Oops, I'm okay. Just fine." She threw herself in, landed sideways, tried to right herself and whacked her elbow on the door handle.

She reached for the seat belt and jerked it across her face. "I can get this."

She pushed it toward the latch and pinched her finger. She yelped and let go, and the belt slapped back into her head. I reached over and buckled her in. She turned to thank me and connected with my chin. I jumped back and fell on my ass.

Belle did an eye roll and got out of the car. She closed the passenger door and pulled me to my feet.

I rubbed my backside and slid behind the wheel. Belle got in and off we went. For two blocks.

"I'm taking dance lessons to help with some problems. A wee bit of addiction, my therapist says. She thinks in-

196

tense physical exercise will keep me focused on other things besides those silly drugs. I think it's working. Maybe it'll help my coordination, too." Valerie tried to casually cross her legs and bumped the seat back hard enough that Belle lurched forward. Valerie paid us and stumbled up the steps into the dance studio.

We had an hour before the next pickup, so we decided to go shopping. It was strange to shop and still keep an eye out for crazy Susan. I was having trouble seeing the Susan I'd had brief contact with as an insane, murdering monster trying to take over her father's crime business.

Belle was having trouble seeing herself in anything besides spandex and glitter.

I handed her a pair of plain brown slacks. "Brown is the new black."

"Those look like shit," Belle said, holding up the pants.

"You haven't tried them on yet."

"No, I mean, they really look like poop. You could stain your pants and no one would notice."

"Maybe that's the advantage. To the brown thing."

"Yeah, with an aging population, incontinence won't show."

Belle finally found a white shirt that didn't hide her boobs, but they weren't overflowing either. And a pair of straight black pants that toned down her silver 3-inch heels. Definitely de-blinged. On the way out we passed the shoe department. I stopped at a pair of gold sparkly stilettos with 6-inch spike heels.

"How do you walk in those?" I ran a finger down the heel.

"Why would you walk in them? They're slut shoes. You don't walk in slut shoes."

"What do you do with them? Where could you wear them without tipping over?"

"Tipping over is the point. You wear those to bed, he's gonna stuff the cannoli with the best chocolate."

My gaze went back to the shoes. I thought about Jon and chocolate. I bet he had superdark and lots of it.

I followed Belle to the car. We headed to Florence Heights for our next fare.

Florence Heights is the alternative to Hampshire Heights. The only height in most public housing is in the name, and this was no exception. Florence Heights is six miles from downtown if you have wings and travel in a straight line. There is no easy, direct driving route to Florence Heights. Most drivers avoid it for the same reasons they avoid Hamp Heights. No tips, long waits, possible violence.

Our guy lived three buildings from the main road. Because Florence Heights was more isolated than Hamp Heights, it had less highway trash in the landscape. The apartment that we pulled up to actually had flowers planted by the door. Maybe the tenant did some gardening.

Maybe not, I thought as a muscular black guy with a shaved head came out. He had on blue jeans that fit with the waist, amazingly, at his waist. He was about 35 and wore a wife-beater T-shirt that showed off tattoos on both arms. One tat said "I'm in love" with no name, leaving his options open. The other said "Here come de judge" and had a tiny scale under it. It wasn't clear whether the scale represented the weighing of justice or drugs.

Belle jumped out and opened the door for him, getting a good look at his package in the process.

"Thanks," he said, smiling. His teeth were way too good for Florence Heights. State-funded dental care was my guess.

He slid in and fastened his seat belt.

"So where you goin'?" Belle asked.

"The courthouse."

"Ah, so, what's your name?"

"Carlton"

"I'm Belle, and this here's Honey. We be at your service and your means of transport for the afternoon. You just tell us what you need and we will make you happy."

I rolled my eyes and poked Belle in the thigh.

For the rest of the ride, Carlton and Belle exchanged stories about the two Heights, comparing living conditions, police attention and general mayhem. The consensus was that they were pretty much the same. If you kept your head down and minded your own business, it wasn't bad. Public transportation was lousy from either.

When we got to the courthouse, Belle and I both got out, expecting someone to meet our fare, a lawyer or a cop, and pay the bill. The only person outside the courthouse entrance was the elderly door guard.

"Mornin', Judge Witherspoon," he greeted Carlton. "Been stayin' at your momma's house again, I see. How is that lovely lady?"

Belle looked at me. Carlton winked at Belle. "Nice meeting you ladies," he said. "Hope we meet again, not in my courtroom, of course." He handed Belle a twenty. "Keep the change. The ride was a great way to start the morning."

"You have got to be kidding." Belle stared after him. "He don't look like any judge I've ever seen."

The guard sidled over to us. "I can always tell when he's visiting his mother. He dresses different. Likes to fit in, I guess. I sure do wish she'd move in with him. But she likes it there. One of the best judges I've seen on the bench in 30 years."

"There goes the judge," Belle grunted. "And I thought I coulda been in love."

"Wait a minute," I said, opening the driver's door. "You were interested when you thought he was a felon. Just because he went to law school and got educated, he's off limits?"

"Well, duh! It's not the education. Hell, I got one of those. It's the law thing, as in which side he's on." Belle looked at me like I was beyond dumb.

"You've got an education? Like how much?"

"I did the college thing. My degree is in government with a minor in social work. Came in handy in my previous line of employment."

I wondered if the judge had assumed as much about Belle and me as we had about him? Big tip, so who cares? I disagreed, but I understood Belle's attitude. She assumed a judge would never be interested in a relationship with a former prostitute, so why waste her time on something that would never happen? It made me wonder if she was really sure that she was done with her former life. But it was interesting to know she'd had a better education than I did.

Ten minutes later, we were back at Cool Rides to see what kind of people-moving Mona had for us.

Mona stuck her head out the door. "Don't bother to get out of the car. I got two more for you. One right now. One in an hour. Short hauls, no conflict, but you'll need to hustle." She handed us the yellow slips with names, locations, destinations and phone numbers.

The first pickup was uptown to the hospital. It was Spike. He was one of our regulars, and his eight-inch mohawk that he gels into spikes and dyes different colors, mood-dependent, had earned him the nickname. He dressed in black leather and chains, with multiple piercings. Visually, he was what you never want your daughter, or your son, to bring home. But the accessory that really stood out with Spike was the baby stroller. The stroller was filled with mini-Spike. An angel of a two-year-old boy with his hair mohawked, spiked and colored to match dad, accompanies Spike everywhere. Spike is a stay-at-home father, and a damn fine one.

Today, he was taking his son to the hospital for a checkup, which probably included shots of some sort.

We dropped them at the ER and off-loaded the stroller, the baby blankets, the pacifiers, the toys, the car seat and the diaper bag. We left them standing next to a pile of gear that would make a mountain climber happy.

"We'll wait for half an hour. If you get done by then, you get half-fare home. Otherwise, we have a pickup in an hour, so we'll have to come back for you."

"Hey, that's great. We'll hustle, right, Samuel?" He leaned over and patted his son on the cheek. The angel giggled.

"Jeez, that is soo cute." Belle watched him walk through the swinging doors. We sat for about five minutes. That doesn't sound like very long. Have you ever tried to sit still with nothing to do for longer than five minutes? It's tough. It's boring. We parked the car in the massive parking lot and began the wait.

"I'm hungry." Belle rolled down her window. "I wonder what they got for hospital food in there."

"Okey dokey," I said. We went through the emergency room filled with screaming children, sniffling and coughing adults and probably a few plague victims and found the breakfast café. It sold doughnuts and coffee. You are what you eat.

We had settled into a booth with our tray of sugar high when a woman in a baggy flowered jumper, a big-brimmed straw hat and sunglasses slipped in next to me. She looked like Annie Hall doing Iowa farm girl. Right off the bus, waiting for the first pimp to commandeer her.

"Long time no see." She slid her glasses down her nose.

"Holy crap." Belle began to slide out of the booth.

It was Susan Young or Susan Scarpelli or whoever she was today.

Chapter 16

"I wouldn't go anywhere." She lifted the cute matching jacket that covered the gun in her hand.

"You wouldn't dare shoot that in here. Besides, you'd ruin that cutesy-wootsy matching jacket." Belle's eyes cut to the empty counter. I had seen the clerk walk off with a plate of doughnuts for her own jean-tightening break.

"Look at it this way. We're in a hospital. If I shoot you, you have a marginally better chance of survival. But I'm a pretty good shot. You probably wouldn't make it to the ER. Dead before you hit the floor. And, personally, I like the matching-jacket thing."

"Just what is it that you want from us? Either of us? What the hell is going on?" I tried to slow down and stall for time. Someone had to come into the coffee shop sooner or later. Sooner would be better. No one would mind seeing that jacket filled with holes, but I hoped I might be missed.

"I just need to clean up a few loose ends. You two are, like, a loose end. Who's going to take me seriously if I can't close the books on a two-bit taxi driver and a whore?"

"You should be in Mexico." Belle settled back on the bench.

"Don't push me. I need to be ruthless if I'm going to take over my father's organization. And I am going to take it. What I don't need is you two mucking around in my way. You're just a means to an end."

"Since you shot Lester, I think the police might be more of a problem than we are. And what end are we a means to?" I crossed my arms and leaned back, too.

"Lester's dead? Well, I sure as hell didn't shoot him." Susan's face paled. I looked at her for a few seconds. Some emotion flashed in her eyes. Pain? Anger, maybe. Or insanity. What kind of relationship had she had with Lester? And could she really not know what had happened to him? Maybe it was Daddy, cleaning house. I doubted that there was any evidence either way. But if it was grief I saw, it passed remarkably quickly.

"Shit," Susan muttered. "This is gonna be harder than I thought."

"Maybe Daddy is a wee bit pissed off." I bit into a cream doughnut. "Did you trash my apartment?" I wanted to know who to worry about, and I didn't see Susan as a long-range planner. She was becoming unpredictable. She probably couldn't shoot both of us, but she didn't seem to care. Her world had shrunk to include herself and herself. Anyone who didn't believe her version of reality was to be dismissed or eliminated. Belle and I fell into the latter category.

"Goddamn right I trashed it. We wanted that disc. It had good information that we didn't want in the wrong hands. And you idiots gave it to the police. How stupid is that?"

"I think I'm being dissed." Belle looked at me. "Do you think I'm being dissed?"

"Hey, I'm not the idiot here. I'm not taking on your father, who happens to be the largest crime boss in the area, trivial as that area is. I keep my head down and my nose clean. And is that the royal we?" I answered Susan.

"Yeah," said Belle. "And I keep my head down. And they never got any evidence about my nose. So maybe some self-examination type of stuff is in order for you, Susan."

"Oh, bugger off." Susan sounded stressed. "The police have nothing on me. I didn't do Lester. And I'm not really taking on my father."

"Hey," said Belle. "What about you keeping me prisoner against my will? That's gotta be illegal somehow."

"Maybe I was held prisoner in my own house. Maybe those other two goons were my father's. Yeah, that could play. Okay, I could go a different direction here. I could just get Daddy locked up. That would work for me. But I still need to do something about you two. You're a blot on my reputation."

I don't think I'd ever been called a blot on someone's reputation.

"You're on your own there. I don't think we can help you."

"You can if little pieces of you start showing up in the right places," said Susan, showing the gun again. "You don't want me to start shooting off rounds in a hospital. I might hit something besides you. So get your asses moving. We are so out of here."

"Can I ask you one more question?" I wanted to keep her where someone might notice us, and provide a distraction.

"Jesus, you are a curious bitch. What now? The shoes?"

"Well, that, too." I paused. "Why did you shoot your husband in the butt, in the courthouse, in broad daylight?"

"Shit, what an asshole he was." Susan's ego was getting the better of her. She wanted to share. I was a good listener.

"He was stepping out on me. I had to show him I could get to him anywhere, any time. I married him because he was working for my father. Who knew he was such an idiot? And such a dud in the sack?"

"Yeah," Belle said, "messing around on the boss's daughter? Dumbsville."

"Who cares about the boss? That was me he was fooling around on. No way was that going to happen. He needed a lesson, big time." Susan grinned. It was a scary thing to see.

"So then you shot him dead? Seems like marriage counseling would have been easier." I kept asking questions. Where the hell was the waitress?

"I didn't shoot him. He stole a few million of Daddy's money and was getting ready to skip town with the cash. That's a no-no in our family."

"Guess he didn't know the rules," said Belle. "Can I ask about Horace? I mean, he wasn't my favorite person, but he seemed pretty loyal to the family. Why'd you shoot him?"

Susan looked exasperated. She sighed and moved the gun to a more visible position.

"You keep asking why I shot people. I hardly ever shoot anyone. I certainly didn't waste ammunition on Horace. Lester and someone were over there looking for the disc. We didn't want it to fall into the wrong hands. Of course, you idiots took care of that. Horace was an accident. He came flying through the window and Lester shot him. I personally would have tortured him and found the disc. But dumb Lester overreacted."

I would have hidden under the table before I would have shot anyone.

"But enough with the questions. Time to go." Susan waved her coat-covered arm toward the entrance.

"And just where are you taking us? Huh? You think you can just walk out of here with two respected members of the community and make them disappear?" said Belle.

"Who? A ho and a taxi driver? Like the community is really going to miss you. I can't even figure out why Willie gives a shit about you. Just hire new drivers. They must be a dime a dozen. But he cares, so here we are."

Voicing my thoughts that a taxi driver or a prostitute is worth twice as much as a lawyer or a mob boss to any sane community seemed counterproductive under the circumstances. The conversation was getting weird, and Susan's motives resembled scrambled eggs, mixed up and well cooked. But she kept talking and, by the time she shut up we had a pretty good idea of where we all stood. She wanted to take over her daddy's business. To do that, she had decided to prove that she could increase the moving of certain product up the interstate. To do that, she'd tried to recruit the Cool Rides Taxi Company. To do that, she had to put some pressure on Willie. We were her pressure. She also needed to know who in her father's organization would back her and who would stick with him. Horace had that information on the disc we had given to the police. No wonder she wanted to shoot us.

As I was trying to find good reasons for Susan not to shoot us, two ambulances roared up to the ER entrance, sirens blaring, brakes screeching. Susan looked at us and fired a round into the floor. The hospital staff was focused on incoming. No one even looked our way. Too much noise to sort out something as mundane as a gunshot.

"Come on, up and at 'em." Susan stood and stepped away from the booth. We all trooped out of the coffee shop and started toward the entrance to the building.

Just as we reached the automatic door, I heard a high-pitched wail and the pounding of many feet.

"Nooo shoots." Mini-Spike tore out the door, flying on spinning 2-year-old legs. And hit Susan in the back of her knees with all the torque his chubby little body could muster. Susan flipped over backward. Her gun went skittering across the floor. Mini-Spike scrambled up and over her, stomping on her stomach, and headed for the door in a blur. Susan started to get up. And big Spike tripped over her, kicking her in the ribs. He mumbled an apology, regained his footing and ran after his son. A nurse followed him and stepped on Susan's hand. An orderly followed the nurse and connected with a foot. When the parade had finally passed, Susan struggled to her feet. Belle was on her stomach in the vicinity where the gun had dropped. I suspected it might be under her spreading bosom.

"You," Susan hissed. "You I will deal with. One way or another, I'll finish this." And she staggered out the door.

My cell phone rang.

"Where the hell are you?"

"Hi, Jon."

"Honey, if I didn't fear for your life right now, I would strangle you. Where are you?"

"I'm at the hospital."

"What? What happened and what's the damage?"

"I'm fine. I was just delivering a fare."

Just then both fares came back in. Spike had his arms wrapped around a kicking, screaming, red-faced Mini-Spike.

"He found out he had to get a shot. I guess he understands more of what we were saying than I thought. Hope your friend is okay." And he slung the child over his shoulder, sack-style, and disappeared back into the ER.

I could hear Jon yelling at the other end of the phone.

"Are we having a fight? Because if we are, I need some comfort food. I have some doughnuts here, but I'm not sure it's enough. I think I need chocolate. And, by the way, Susan Scarpelli stopped by the hospital to say hi."

I could hear Jon sighing on the other end of the phone. "Do you need any help?"

"Not unless you want to corral a 2-year-old who just learned the word shot."

"Shot what? A 2-year-old shot someone?" His voice was rising again, by an octave or two.

"Shot, as in what the doctor gives you. We're headed back to Cool Rides as soon as Spike finishes getting Mini-Spike inspected."

"We need to talk. I need to know what Susan was doing at the hospital. We have a warrant out for her as a witness."

"Yeah, we need to share information. And accommodations and stuff like that."

"Stuff?"

"I have another fare in 15 minutes. Gotta go." I flipped the phone closed.

"Is hot buns about to come roaring in with his bubble light screaming?"

"The bubble light doesn't scream. That's the siren." I slid down the wall until I was sitting next to Belle.

"I know that. I was speaking metaphorically."

"No, he's not. I don't think." And it was true. Right now I couldn't think. I needed to get back to Cool Rides. Safe ground for me.

Belle stood up. She had Susan's gun in her hand. "Let's go." She tucked it in her oversized bag and offered me a hand up. "Here come Spike and Mini. We got another fare to pick up. Time's a-wastin'."

We dropped Spike and Mini downtown. Mini had apparently made his peace with his father, or he had just worn himself out. His hair was pretty flat. I wondered how long it would take Spike to redo the do.

Belle pulled out the next fare slip.

"Well, look at this. I know this woman. She's in the business."

"As in your ex business?"

"Yeah, she's a ho. Her client base is mainly in Springfield, but last I knew, she was building up a pretty good local constituency. You know that 'buy local' ad campaign? She could be the poster girl for that."

"I'm not sure that's what they had in mind. Where are we picking her up?"

"Swing this chariot around to Crescent Street. She's meeting someone at The Streetside Café."

"Whoa, swank. Business must be pretty good."

"Sweetie pie, that business is always doing good. But it can wear you out fast. I just outgrew it."

"Or maybe found out how scary it can be."

"Yeah, that, too. Hey, you got any kind of self-defense in that undersize suitcase you carry?"

"Like?"

"Like anything. Gun, stun gun, pepper spray, big dildo?"

"Big what? How would a big dildo defend me?"

"Girl, use your imagination. How'd you get Bozo's attention when we were locked up at Susan's condo?"

"I grabbed his balls."

"Exactly. Think how much more effective a big old dildo would have been. And then you could have whacked him over the head with it. And … it still would have been perfectly good for later use."

File that one away for future defense. I didn't even own a dildo. Or a gun or a stun gun. I did have some pepper spray. "So, what have you got in your bag?"

"What haven't I got? I got Susan's gun, which we never told the lieutenant about, right? And I got a bottle of hair spray." Belle dug around in her purse. "And I got some pepper spray and a pair of brass knuckles. And a big ol' dildo."

"You have a dildo in there? No, you're shitting me."

"Take a gander." And Belle pulled out the biggest penis I have ever seen not attached to an elephant. It was encased in a clear plastic box lined with blue silk. I almost drove off the road.

"Stop distracting me. The original of that must have belonged to a horse."

"Yeah, it can make a strong man feel mighty inadequate. That's a pretty good self-defense right there."

I slowed the cab and took a right turn. Crescent Street is a very upscale neighborhood next to Smith College. It houses mostly Smith professors and professionals who work in Northampton and the surrounding area. There are a number of apartments for rent in the larger houses. Belle's friend from the business lived in one of these.

I gulped when she came out. Elegant, striking, with long blond hair and legs that stopped somewhere north of the pole. She was dressed in a silk suit that would have been at home on any CEO in any boardroom in any capital-ist country. Prostitution certainly was paying well, and the wardrobe was a different approach from Belle's. It was obvious who was in charge in her client relationships. She walked to the car with a stride that was graceful, commanding and feminine all at the same time. I wondered how long she had practiced that walk before she got it right. Did she take lessons? Could I take lessons?

"Honey, this is Charlotte. She graduated from Smith five years ago and decided to put her degree to work. There's nothing like good networking."

"Hey, Belle. I heard you hadn't been in circulation for a while. Sorry about Horace, I guess."

"Yeah, no one deserves to die early. But he came pretty damn close. I got tired of the life. I'm giving cab driving a whirl."

"Whatever floats," Charlotte replied. She had a wonderfully cultured, very deep voice. I could see her giving public-speaking lessons. But, like she said, whatever floats.

I pulled up in front of the café. Charlotte exited with the grace of being born to money. I wondered what the psychological implications of her profession were. In her case, I'd bet money was not a motivating factor.

"Why do you figure she works as a prostitute?" I asked Belle after Charlotte had entered the restaurant.

"Why not? Nothing wrong with it as a job goes. Pays well. Flexible hours. I didn't mind it. I just got bored. And what with Horace eliminated from the management position, it seemed like a good time to let it go. Besides, in Charlotte's case, she had a lot to prove. Like that she likes being called 'she', but 'she' isn't. And letting her off here reminds me that it's lunchtime. I need something besides doughnuts to sustain me."

"What do you mean, 'she' isn't? She isn't what?"

"She isn't a she. Decided against the surgical option. She still has balls."

"No! She went to Smith College. She's a prostitute, for God's sake."

"God didn't have anything to do with it, and Smith doesn't require a DNA test. They just assume. And she's a damn fine ho. She just has a specialized technique. Does some dominatrix stuff and lots of mouth-to-crotch resuscitation. A little hand action. You know the saying?"

"No, don't tell me. Is this some kind of special ho proverb?"

"Yeah, but anyone can use it. A little hand, a little tongue, whee, all done!"

"Too much information!" I yelped. Why did I ask about these things?

I thought about Charlotte. I thought about men and wondered how many of her clients knew. Then I let it go. Belle was right. I needed food, too. "Okay, food."

"I hear a burger calling my name. And fries. And maybe a hot fudge sundae." Belle grinned. "Packard's?"

Packard's is a local bar that serves the ultimate hamburger. It's stuffed with jalapeño peppers, which are stuffed with pepper jack cheese. Then it's dipped in a beer batter and deep-fried. It ain't rabbit food.

I called into Cool Rides to see if Mona had anything for us. She had an airport fare at 2 o'clock, so now was a good time for lunch.

At 1:30 we rolled into Cool Rides, stomachs sated and arteries clogged. The next two hours were an uneventful ride to the airport. Unless you count our fare being stopped and searched by the feds before he even got into the terminal. But he had already paid and tipped us, so it doesn't count in my book. His book is probably different.

We got back to Cool Rides around 3:30. Mona gave us six more short hauls. By 5:30, Andrew had reported in to start some late-night airport and train runs. I was glad he was a night person. The 10-after-10 train from New Haven was usually at least an hour late. In an effort to maintain our own reputation for being on time and super reliable, we always went to Springfield at the scheduled time to meet it and always sat for an hour or more. That usually meant the driver getting home around midnight. Too late if you started work at 9 in the morning. Andrew was somehow able to turn off his excessive energy and sleep while he waited for his passengers. I needed to be in my own bed.

Belle and I headed back to Jon's house so Belle could cook. She wouldn't discuss details, but dinner was going to be made.

"I'm going to go next door and ask Lucille if she wants some dinner," I said. What I really meant was that Belle hadn't made any dessert and I would bet my sexiest underwear that Lucille would have plenty of something made with sugar. She handed me one of her giant platters and we popped back to Jon's side.

Jon arrived at 6:30 to the smell of lemon chicken, herbed rice, and broccoli with hollandaise sauce. I'd set the table, which told me that I was bordering on domestic. I wondered if Jon noticed and how he felt about having so much live-in help. Apparently, he was comfortable enough with it to sit down and devour the food.

When we had all finished and cleared, Jon leaned back in his chair and eyed me speculatively.

"We need to talk about the Scarpellis. Both of them." He tipped his chair down with a thud.

Belle rose and headed toward the bedrooms.

"You, too. Don't even think about skipping out tonight." He pointed at Belle.

Lucille smiled her usual beatific smile and sat with a sort of vacant look in her eyes. I was beginning to realize that Lucille's facial expression and her brain activity were extremely separated. I suspected that her mind was two steps ahead of mine at all times.

Belle returned to her chair and sat.

"I'm having trouble fitting some of the pieces of this father-daughter relationship together. I need to know more about what she said to you at the hospital." Jon looked from me to Belle.

I tried to think back to her nasty comments about us being bad for her reputation. Did that mean she wanted to kill us so that she would be taken seriously? Was she dealing with reality if she thought she could oust her father? He'd been in business for a long time. Those kinds of loyalties aren't built fast or easily. Maybe she just wanted an entry into the male-dominated hierarchy of the business. Her father didn't seem overly concerned about the disc being in the hands of the police. The most it could do for the police was tell them who to watch, inside and outside the blue brotherhood.

Lucille refocused her eyeballs and turned to Jon.

"The only thing that makes these incidents related is the people. We have three shootings: Horace, Susan's husband

and Lester Cardozzo. We have Honey's apartment trashed. We have kidnapping. We have a visit from Mr. Scarpelli. Maybe the motivations for the shootings are unrelated and the rest of the incidents are collateral damage."

At the mention of Mr. Scarpelli, Jon frowned. He was still mad that we'd let him into the house. I wasn't sure how I felt about being collateral damage.

"We have a confrontation with Susan," Lucille finished.

"I think we know why Susan shot her husband." Belle sort of mumbled this. She had a natural aversion to giving information to the police. The police in question stared at her.

"And are we going to share this?"

"Keep your pants creased, pal. Yeah, we can share. Susan said her husband was stepping out on her. He was cheating. She didn't seem to like him anyway and he wasn't very good where it counted."

"Did she say whether she hired someone to kill him? As long as she was confessing to you, I mean."

I coughed. "She wanted him to know that she could get to him anywhere, any time, so she picked the most public, secure place she could think of. It worked. He was terrified of her. He embezzled money from her father to get away."

"And ended up dead anyway. We know she didn't actually kill him. That was probably Daddy," I added. "She also said that Horace was shot by accident. That's what Belle's friend said. He went flying through the window and Lester overreacted a bit."

Jon drummed his fingers on the table. "So Lester's murder was just housecleaning by Scarpelli. Nothing we can ever prove. And, thank God, not in my jurisdiction."

217

Lucille said, "So that accounts for all the bodies. But why was Susan so determined to threaten Belle and Honey? Even Scarpelli didn't seem all that concerned about the disc going to the police. There's something else going on here. Something that Susan wants. I think the taxi company is at the center of it. She didn't come after Belle until after Belle started driving for Cool Rides. And they went after Honey before they went after Belle."

"Maybe the disc was a fuckup by Susan. Whatever was on it pissed her father off. Now she's trying to redeem herself," I said, but it still didn't seem right to me. "Anyway, Susan is the one in the middle of it. I think Lucille is right. Susan said some stuff about using Cool Rides. I think she and Daddy may have a difference of opinion over that. But she wants to take over the Scarpelli operations, I think."

"We just have to find her," Jon said. "I got a search warrant for her office. That wasn't easy. Attorneys are more protected than a Wall Street banker. She may not have killed anyone yet, but I think she could get away with it if she decides to." He grimaced. "Honey, you and Belle need to stay safe. I don't think you're taking this seriously enough."

What Jon didn't know was that I had passed beyond serious and advanced to hysteria mode. If Susan Scarpelli could walk into a courtroom and shoot someone, she sure as hell could get to me when she wanted to. Sometimes I felt like I had the street smarts of Bambi. Susan hadn't had much luck yet, so maybe she was due.

"How does Scarpelli make a living?" Everyone looked at me blankly. "Everyone has to file a tax return. What's he claim is his income source?"

Jon grinned. "Porta Potties. He has some trucks and a bunch of shit houses. He moves them around to construction sites. The feds have looked at his books. Never found anything they could nail him for."

"So, then, what's his real source of income?" I asked.

"Transportation." Jon leaned back in his chair. "He owns the Route 91 corridor between Hartford, Connecticut, and the Canadian border. Northampton is a big stop because of the five colleges. He doesn't actually deal anything illegal. He just transports and distributes it to the second-tier dealers."

"Something we have in common. I'm in the transportation business, too. Just more legitimate. And limited to people." We all pondered that for a minute. "What's he use to move stuff now?"

"We've never been able to get a handle on it. Maybe his trucks, but we've used every excuse we could to stop and search and never found anything. No one ever volunteers for that duty. Moving shit in Porta Potties would make some sense. Might damage the product. Not that the crack heads would notice." Jon sighed. "I guess I better talk to Willie tomorrow. Lucille may be right. Scarpelli needs to expand and Cool Rides would be good cover. Did Willie ever mention anything like pressure being put on him?"

"Not to me, but Mona would be the one to ask. She and Willie are pretty tight. They share a lot." I said, glaring at Jon. "Susan sure thought she was putting pressure in the right place."

Jon looked at Belle. "What about the other cab company?"

"Lucky's Limo? All I ever did was get rides to Holyoke and Springfield. Sometimes with Horace. Sometimes not. They never stopped anywhere else when I was in the car."

"Did Horace stay with the car or get out with you?"

"He usually stayed with the car. They would just drop me off. I called for a pickup when I was done. I don't know where they went."

"So, we have a mobster who controls the transportation of illegal goods up and down the interstate. There's an in-family disagreement about who's in charge of the business and how to expand. We have a lot of threats and violence against the drivers for a local taxi company that travels that interstate. And no proof of anything more sinister than that," said Lucille.

"Susan slapped me around. They took me against my will." Belle looked indignant.

"They threatened me with a gun," I added.

"At least one of the guys who threatened you is dead. Safe to assume that he was the one who shot Horace. He's not in my jurisdiction anyway. We're left with Susan's husband. She's got an alibi. Daddy's cleaning up her mess." Jon drummed his fingers again. "What's on your agenda tomorrow?" He looked at me and then at Belle. Maybe he had finally given up on the control issue.

"I'm driving. Belle and I could still stick together. Cuts into the income, but we might both survive to spend it."

"Yeah, I'm up for that," said Belle.

We'd been talking for over an hour and had theories about the three murders but no proof. Lucille's idea made the most sense. Talking to Mona and Willie might help. I knew that most small cities in the country had some drug dealing. Northampton, apparently, had more than others because of the interstate and the large student population. Mona found hypodermic needles in the flowerpots in front of the Cool Rides garage on a regular basis. I had seen an occasional junkie nodding off uptown. Once in a while there was a drug-related death reported in the local news. But most of the drug problems seemed to stay to the south, in the larger cities. Maybe the evil side of drug use was moving into our little neighborhood. Now I knew who might be responsible for the delivery of that to the city's front door.

Lucille decided it was her bedtime and left for next door. Belle said she had a book and disappeared into the bedroom. Jon's cell phone rang.

"Stevens." He sighed into it. It had been a long day and his was probably about to get longer. "Yeah, okay." Police lieutenants had to be available for a lot of hours. After a day of B&E, traffic stops too numerous to count, medical and well-being checks, slashed tires and trespassing notices, they called him in on a domestic violence. There was a restraining order and a warrant out on the woman involved, and she had a teddy bear clutched in her arms that she wouldn't give up. Patrol decided Jon should come in and take it away.

He rose and went to the door. "Don't wait up. I'll find my way to the bedroom." And he was out the door.

My existence was becoming emotionally taxing. Understanding Susan's psychotic reasoning was way beyond my capacity. My brain was nearing meltdown and needed a rest. I headed for bed.

Chapter 17

I woke up at 8 o'clock. Time to hustle. I was in the kitchen guzzling coffee when Belle wandered in.

"You checked in with Mona yet to see if we got anything for this morning?"

"No," I said and handed her the cell phone. She punched in the short code for Cool Rides. Number 1.

I heard Mona's voice on the other end and Belle groaned. She hadn't been involved in the company for very long, but she had already met most of the regulars.

"We have to pick up Denise. She wants a ride from her place in the Meadows."

Denise was one of our occasional regulars. She called every two to four weeks wanting a ride to one of the cheap motels out on the old highway. There were three of these and she could always count on one of them to have a room available. None of the upscale, in-town hotels would take her. Most were too expensive anyway. We all kind of liked Denise. She tipped well and was always entertaining. It was just that we had to drive with all the windows down and the air conditioning on full blast, and we had to detail the car when we got back to the garage. We still ended up using one of those sprays that smell marginally better than a dead ashtray.

The Meadows is a section of Northampton made up mostly of farms, forest and the Connecticut River. It also contains a small airport and the three-county fair-grounds. There are a few houses in the Meadows, but the city planner, in a fit of "not in my back yard-ism," passed rules forbidding any new building in the area. The result is a large piece of land that is unpopulated by permanent structures. It provides ideal spaces for wildlife, drug deals, drunk college students and a camping site for the homeless population convenient to downtown and all their sources of income. Street begging was Denise's favorite source. She lived with her brother and another man in a tent with an ancient propane stove inside and a campfire outside. It was the campfire, and lack of a bathing facility, that made us air out the cab after a Denise ride.

"She wants to be picked up at 9." Belle poured coffee.

At a quarter to 9, Belle and I loaded ourselves into the cab. Jon had gone to work before either of us got up, and Lucille must have been busy. We didn't smell anything worth breaking down her door for, so we headed to the Meadows.

Denise's castle was an old Army tent. It could house six people, so room wasn't an issue. Privacy was. The outhouse was several acres of woods between the tent and the Connecticut River. The bathing facilities were nonexistent. Once a month, Denise would save up enough dimes, nickels and quarters for a bath and a bed.

We pulled up on the dirt road about 50 feet from the tent and honked the horn. This would have been considered bad manners with any other fare. We always walk to the door and knock. If that fails to get them out, we call on the cell phone. Denise didn't have a cell phone. She would arrange her rides the day before, when she was in town working the sidewalks. Given the lack of privacy, we never approached the tent or the area around it. I had done that once. I found her brother sitting with his back against a tree five feet from the tent. He was bare-assed and taking a giant dump. He grinned and waved his penis at me. I retreated to the taxi and sat with all the doors locked until Denise came out.

Apparently, the morning toiletries were over. Denise trotted down the path to the road and slid into the backseat.

"Forward, James, or make that Jamette." Denise was looking chipper and wide awake. Her hair was combed and she 'gasp' was wearing mascara.

"Got myself married last night," she said without any other lead-up to the story. "The old man – well, the new old man – is already out at the North Prince Motel. Hitched a ride there with one of the farmers. I told him I'd join him once I got my face done."

"You look lovely, Denise," Belle said.

"Yeah, well, ever the blushing bride. I needed to get away from the brother for a while. He's such a prick. I tried to get the cops to haul his ass. There's a warrant out. But they could care less about that shit."

"What's the warrant for?" I couldn't help myself. I always got sucked into her stories.

"Oh, just 30 days for an open container."

"That's probably not a priority for them. They have a lot on their minds these days." Like a few murders.

"I coulda told them about the murder," Denise mused. "But I called the FBI instead. They told me to call the staties."

"Did you?" I glanced over my shoulder at her, wondering if Denise could have seen one of the murders currently on Jon's agenda. Or if she was talking about one of the other homeless folks who might have crossed her brother once too often. Would anyone in authority in Northampton notice if a member of its homeless population suddenly didn't show up for work? Given Denise's source of income, most of the population of Northampton probably wished she would miss a day at work begging on the streets.

"Nah, I got bored with it. He wasn't worth the trouble. Anyway, now I got my honey to keep me busy."

"Yeah, guys'll do that to you," Belle said, looking at me.

"What?" I asked.

Denise, oblivious to Belle and me, continued her train of thought.

"I thought they might want to know that he murdered a guy and dumped him in the Ashfield Lake. Wrapped him right up in one of our best blankets. Stones, bungee cords and – plop – right in the lake. Yup."

How do you answer that? "Did you see this happen?" I thought I would at least see how much might be real.

And how much was her attempt to get rid of her brother. Sibling rivalries – one never knew.

"Well, duh. Of course I saw it. Bodies sure do look white when they're dead."

"Denise, maybe you should tell the Ashfield police, or maybe someone right here in Northampton."

"Nah, they all think I'm crazy. 'Sides, I don't bother them, they don't bother me."

"But you did call the FBI."

"Did I say that? Well, maybe I did, maybe I didn't."

I gave up questioning. I could tell Jon what she said. Leave the ball in his court. There were enough bodies floating around in my mind. And where was Susan hiding? I couldn't believe the Springfield police hadn't turned her up at Daddy's house. Unless Daddy had disowned her or worse. But she was his sole heir. Even if she was a woman, she was a Scarpelli woman. How much did family mean to the old man?

My train of thought stopped there because we pulled up in front of the North Prince Motel. There were only two other cars parked in front of rooms, so there was plenty of space for Denise. Her new "husband" had probably already rented the room. But I told her I would wait while she talked to the office lady. Sometimes, if they were mostly rented or if they had had a good week, they would turn her away. Whether they let her rent a room depended on how much they needed her cash. They would have a major cleanup after she left. Denise pulled a wad of money out of her loose pants pockets and peeled off a 20-dollar bill.

"Keep the change. Do I know how to tip or what?" She must have had $500 in the wad. It was a 10-dollar fare.

Belle got out of the car. "Must have had too much coffee. I'll be right back." She went into the lobby to find the restroom. Denise followed her in.

I sighed and slouched in the seat. I yawned. I stretched. I closed my eyes and felt the warmth of the sun on my face. I decided to call Jon, maybe to mention what Denise had told me. Or, if I were honest, just to hear his voice. Speed dial is great. I pushed the number 3 button and put the phone on speaker mode.

"Stevens."

"Hi, lieutenant of the cute butt."

"I sure hope this is Reverend Mother Mary from my high school days."

"We're about to head back to Cool Rides. We just dropped Denise off at the North Prince Motel. I have a good story about that." I sighed and leaned back to enjoy more sunshine.

When the car door opened, I pushed myself up to a sitting position, opening my eyes as I reached to turn the key ... and saw Susan sitting in the passenger seat with a very large gun. She certainly had a good supply of those ugly things.

"Hi, Honey, I'm back. And, by the way, Belle has been detained. This was not the smartest place to come. Amazing how easy it is to get crazy people to be sane for just long enough to do what you've paid them to do."

"You bribed Denise?" I tried for as much outrage as I could muster. That was about as low as Susan had gone so far. Denise was crazy and unpredictable. But, it seemed, so was Susan. She had clearly lost the powers of logical thought.

"I gave her and her new idiot a wedding present. It was the least I could do."

"So, now what? You want to make your bones on me?"

"Oh, Honey, you've been watching too many Godfather movies. Anyway, bones or no bones, I'm not going to shoot you dead and dump you in a nice, smelly toilet, if that's what you're worried about. And I promise I won't put a dead horse in your bed. Come to think of it, that might be an improvement for you." I didn't like the detail that she provided. Lester Cardozzo had been dumped in a toilet.

"Then what the hell is going on? What are you trying to do?" I asked.

"I'm just trying to finish up. The board of directors assigned me a project, and I need to make a completed presentation next week."

"A project? I'm a project?" I answered dumbly.

"Yeah. I'm supposed to enhance the possibilities of transportation along the 91 interstate corridor between Hartford and the northern border of Vermont. We've reached maximum capacity with our current carriers. We need to expand. And Cool Rides is the ideal expansion associate. But we need some cooperation here, and Willie isn't providing it. Are you getting my drift here?"

"You want me to convince him to join your project."

"Oh, Honey, you are so perceptive. You might make partner yet. Belle is just going to sit tight with my friend in there while you and I go for a ride."

Leaning forward, I gave my brain a silent pep talk and started the car. Don't panic. Stay calm until you can't.

"Where to?"

"Cool Rides, of course."

"What are you going to do when we get there?" I hadn't expected her to go into such a public place.

"I'm going to give Willie a contract. Then I'm going to call my friend in there" – she waved her hand at the motel office – "and tell him to chop off one of those beautifully manicured fingers that Belle loves so well. Every hour until the contract gets signed, he'll get another finger. Special delivery, by taxi."

I gurgled and hit the gas.

We arrived at Cool Rides 10 minutes later. There were no cars in front of the garage, and the office seemed overly quiet. There should have been coming and going, phones ringing, people stopping in. I knew this, but Susan didn't have the rhythm of the company hardwired into her brain the way I did.

My hand went up in an automatic gesture to grab the phone. Cool Rides runs on cell phones, so the drivers take them everywhere. When you're sitting on the toilet, the phone sits next to you. You never, never leave them in the car.

Flipping it down, I shoved it into my pocket and got out of the car cautiously. Susan looked at me. "I've got a very large gun under this coat, Honey, and I'll use it. Probably on Willie first. He's been such a pain in the ass. Maybe that would be the most efficient thing to do. So behave yourself."

I raised my hands over my head and turned to the office door.

"Oh please, enough with the theatrics. This is a fucking business meeting, not the final episode of The Sopranos. Just walk in like you're checking for another fare."

I lowered my hands and tried to see what was going on inside the building. Not much, as near as I could tell.

Mona was in the office cubicle, her head bent over papers on the desk. Willie was probably in the garage. I was on high alert, adrenaline pumping, absorbing details I'd never noticed. The unisex bathroom door was cracked open. The door from the office/waiting area to the garage was the same. There was silence from the garage. Even without the tools crashing and the machines buzzing, the radio was usually ear splittingly loud.

Susan walked to the office. She looked at Mona. "Go find Willie or Mona will lose a kneecap." She said into my ear.

I wasn't sure how crazy Susan was. I decided to assume completely.

"So, where's Willie?" I tried to lean casually against the door.

"Garage," Mona replied without looking up.

Susan gestured me in that direction with the coat. I would never think of jackets as just an accessory again.

Willie came through the garage door, looked up and saw Susan. His expression changed, and a wave of hatred crossed his face as he walked toward the office.

"Susan," he said, "I thought we agreed that you wouldn't come around here again."

"Aren't you cute today? We didn't agree to anything. That's the problem here. We need to agree that I'm not going to change the shape of Honey's face. Or Mona's knees. Or Belle's hands. Or just put a fucking hole in your head. We need an understanding and a contract."

Willie looked around. "Where is Belle?"

"Oh, Belle's hands are in good hands. They have a great big ax." She paused. "So let's negotiate."

"Just what is it that you want from Cool Rides?" Willie was talking too loud.

"I need a contract that says you will service whatever I need transported up the interstate corridor. I need your assurance that you understand exactly what the consequences will be if you say no again. And our business needs 50 percent of your business. You will be paid extremely well."

Willie shifted his weight forward. Mona rolled her chair closer. I stood like a stone. Although the "paid extremely well" had not escaped my notice.

"What part does your father play in this?" Willie asked.

"Ah, dear old Dad. No ambition. You could run a truck, or a taxi, through his company and he wouldn't notice. It needs new blood. That would be me."

"Why not just increase his truck fleet? Use them." Willie was almost screaming now.

"Too obvious. They get searched every time they take a load of shit somewhere."

"Why me? Why not Lennie's limo, or Larry's, or Lulu's or whatever the hell it is?"

Susan looked at him like he was the stupidest person on earth. "Because, Mr. Country Hick, they are at capac-

232

ity. We load them up any more and somebody is going to notice. I can't believe they haven't been busted yet. Nope, Cool Rides is the cleanest operation around. It's just perfect for our expansion plans. Now sign the damn contract." She pulled a single sheet of paper from her jacket and placed it on the table.

I couldn't believe that Susan thought a contract signed under this kind of duress was going to change anything. She might have to kidnap one of us permanently just to make this work. I wondered what her daddy thought. Maybe she thought none of us would go to the police. Maybe this was all in her head and Daddy had no expansion plans at all. So many maybes, so little sanity.

"Hey, Susan," I said, "does the other cab company have a contract? Luther's, or Lars' or Lola's or whatever? Because, if they do, I want to see it. I mean, just how much is this worth to you? What are you giving them? I think Cool Rides should at least be at the same rate. Don't you, Mona? Willie?"

I was stalling for time, and I think Susan knew it. But her ego, or her insanity, was in charge. "I'm a lawyer, for Christ's sake. You think I don't know how to write a contract?"

"Yeah, but do the drivers get danger wages?" I decided to keep her going as long as I could.

"The biggest danger right now is that I might blow some vital piece of your body off. Willie, sign on the line." She extended a well-chewed fingernail toward the piece of paper.

Just then the phone rang. "Pick it up. And put it on speaker. You're not taking any fares right now."

Mona punched the speaker button and lifted the receiver. "Cool Rides."

"Yo, Cool Rides yourself. You tell Miss Lawyer woman that she is not long for this world. I don't take kindly to threats against my wonderful fingers. I just got a full-scale manicure two days ago."

"Urp." Susan turned a shade of red. "What the fuck? Let me talk to Benji."

"Your goons? Oh, they are so tied up right now. And their ability to converse with you is limited. They got some gray sticky stuff all over their faces … and other parts of their bodies."

Duct tape.

"Belle, I have a gun here. And I have Honey and Mona and Willie. So don't do anything fucking stupid. Not that you can help it. But I will reconfigure someone's body here."

I was still toward the back of the office. I caught a movement in my peripheral vision. The bathroom door had opened a larger crack. I saw Jon's face in the shadow. Maybe it was time to distract Susan. Jon should be able to get behind her with a minimum of movement from me. I could see his gun in his hand.

I started to cough. I grabbed my chest and staggered closer to Susan. She moved in front of me, dropping her coat. She raised the gun, carefully staying between me and the door out of the office.

"Don't think I won't shoot, Honey. I'd love to see you with one less leg." Her back was to the bathroom now. Jon cracked the door open another few inches. He slipped out and moved toward the office door. He took another step. He was behind Susan. Mona and Willie didn't react. They knew he was there. I understood why the office was so quiet. My cell phone. Jon had heard it all. We all kept our eyes focused on Susan.

Belle's voice echoed back into the office. It seemed too loud in the silence. "I don't give a crap what you do there. I'll find you and your life will be hell. No one messes with my new nails."

Jon was behind Susan. He raised his gun and pressed it against Susan's neck. Willie and Mona fell to the floor. I watched in horrified fascination as my hand reached out, all by itself, in slow motion, and slapped Susan's gun. It flew in a graceful arc out the office door, landed with a thud and shot the soda machine. The door wrenched open and soda cans flew in every direction. I hit the floor with Mona and Willie. My autopilot went out. By the time I peeked over the top of the desk, Jon was snapping handcuffs on a screeching Susan.

"You fucking asshole. Do you know what you've done? I'm Susan Scarpelli. No one messes with a Scarpelli. My father will cut you up into little pieces. The Connecticut River will be polluted with your body parts for years. I'll carve your dick off and cook it for dinner." She struggled in Jon's grip. He calmly pulled her arms higher behind her back. Ouch.

"I will get you. Sometime, somewhere, when you aren't looking for it – kablooey! I will shove a stick of dynamite so far up your ass your testicles will come out your nose." Susan's voice had reached a higher pitch than I thought humanly possible. I had to give her some credit for creative threats.

My own opinion was that daddy Scarpelli might be very relieved that Susan was not in circulation anymore. But what did I know about their relationship? What Susan might be able to do from a jail cell was questionable, especially if Daddy wasn't inclined to help.

Jon had his phone out. Seconds later, four uniformed officers were dragging a kicking, screaming Susan to a squad car. I stood up and grabbed Jon by the ears and kissed him on the mouth as hard as I could. Then I did a little dance and raised my fists above my head.

Jon, Willie, Mona and I were sitting in the waiting room, letting our adrenaline fade, when Belle stormed in. "What the hell happened here? I need input. I need all the stuff. What did you do with the bitch? I'm gonna rip her fingers off."

"Hi, Belle. Good to see you again." Jon smiled his thousand-watt smile.

"Good to see me, my ass. I thought driving a taxi would be safe. After life in the business. Being a ho is easy compared to this shit."

"Yeah, but this is more fun," I said. "How is the North Prince?"

"The North Prince still has most of their fingers and toes. Barely. They may never get a manicure again, though."

Jon smiled. "Plenty of uniforms out there?"

"Oh, yeah, like they were lots of help. Excitement was all over by the time they got there. Next time send them a little earlier." She plopped herself down next to Willie. "What kind of pizza we havin'?"

Susan had, apparently, neglected to figure in size and street smarts when she hired the North Prince staff to subdue Belle. Belle had read the situation when she walked in the door and had Benji on his back with a gun in his face before he could even point the gun Susan had given him in the right direction. To his credit, Susan had shown him a fake police ID and told him he would be aiding the cause of peace and love if he locked Belle in the back room. I doubt that her fingers were in any real danger, certainly not from Benji. But when he mentioned Susan's plan, Belle immediately duct-taped him to the reception desk. He didn't understand that torture isn't standard police procedure in this country. He was confessing to crimes that hadn't been committed, or possibly even thought about, yet. Belle had been trying to shut him up when the police cars arrived.

Chapter 18

Three long days later, I was sitting on Jon's couch scarfing pizza and beer and watching football. Jon was admiring game strategy and players' skills. I was admiring butts and tats. It had been three days of filling out paperwork, sitting in interviews with the feds and flopping exhausted into bed at night. My bed. I had officially moved back into my apartment, but Jon had a better (by a lot) TV. And he had pizza and beer. And he had himself. Belle had met a friend from the days of her previous profession and decided to ask her over for some reminiscing. I didn't think Jon would tolerate a night of girlie talk about Belle's good old days. I handed her a key to my cleaner-than-it-had-ever-been-before apartment. She smirked when she told me she would spend the night there.

Susan's lawyer convinced a judge to declare her unfit for trial. The feds had busted her on charges that were beyond my understanding. Threatening a police officer was at the bottom of the long list of charges. Somewhere below that was something to do with her intimidation of Belle and me. No surprise there. Her father hadn't objected to the declaration of unfitness. It would make it almost impossible to trace any of the intimidation stuff back to him. He had probably paid off the judge to agree that she was nuts, or, realistically, he probably didn't have to. She tried to be her own lawyer, but the same judge declared her unfit for that, too. She hadn't actually done any violence to anyone except shooting her husband's butt. Since he was beyond pressing charges and Susan was officially crazy, she would spend long time in the state mental hospital. Everyone agreed that Lester Cardozzo had accidentally killed Horace. The real pisser in all this was that I never found out about the red shoes. Susan will probably go to her grave without revealing that source. The depressing part was that it was unlikely that there was any change in the flow of drugs up the interstate corridor. Cool Rides Cabs won't contribute to the distribution effort, but that probably didn't slow it down much. The other cab companies might find themselves getting pulled over more often. Where there's a market, there will be a supply. My support of total legalization was not an attitude widely shared.

Of course, there was no evidence anywhere about who might have killed Lester. Belle had declined to testify about her kidnapping. She still couldn't tolerate being in a room with uniformed police and a courtroom was completely beyond her. She put up with Jon only because he had a great kitchen, a big-screen TV and a free bedroom. I put up with him because he had a great body and knew how to use it to my satisfaction. At least, I hoped he did. We hadn't done the deed yet. I had high hopes for that night.

When the score was lopsided enough to stop watching, Jon picked up the pizza box and beer bottles. I grabbed the dirty paper towels and followed him to the kitchen. After depositing the garbage on the counter, he turned around. The towels fluttered to the floor.

We made our way backward, kissing and groping, to the bedroom. My pulse rate was higher than when Susan had held a gun to my head. I guess that sums up Jon's effect on me pretty well. We stumbled through the bedroom door and were rolling around on the bed when bells started ringing.

The earth might have been moving, too, but it wasn't Jon's technique that was ringing bells. There are a handful of people who always answer their cell phones. Doctors, firefighters, police, moms. And, unfortunately, Cool Rides taxi drivers. Our phones were screaming for attention separately, together.

We both flipped our phones open. We both heard "Get your ass in here now."

Epilogue

Three hours later I staggered into Jon's house. It felt like I had transported the entire Smith College field hockey team home. Oh yeah, because I had. Their bus had broken down and Cool Rides had to send its entire fleet of cars to gather them up and bring them across the river.

I tossed my keys onto the counter. There was a large gift box lying there with a pink bow and a card. Of course, I had to read the card. Maybe it was for me. How would I know if I didn't read it?

"Good luck!" It read. No name, no signature. It might have been for me. Just as I was thinking about opening it, Jon walked in.

"Where did that come from?" He eyed the box.

"I don't know. I just got here. It was on the counter when I walked in." I put my hand out to pull the bow.

"No, wait," said Jon. "You didn't bring it, and I sure as hell didn't leave it here." He circled it.

"Did you touch it?" He looked at me.

"I read the card."

"What's it say?"

"Good luck."

"I'm calling the bomb squad." Jon turned toward the phone. "Too much stuff has happened in the last three days. If Scarpelli isn't feeling like revenge, Susan sure as hell is. And I don't know what kind of contacts she has."

I backed up a few steps while Jon punched in speed dial. "No sirens," he said as he ended the conversation.

"Why wake up the neighborhood?" he grumbled. "Let's go outside and wait."

Five minutes later a big truck lumbered up and three men in space suits jumped out. A squad car with two more uniforms followed. Jon pointed over his shoulder at the house.

"It's on the kitchen counter."

The first space suit through the door left it open, so of course we had to watch from a substantial distance. They approached the box from three sides. They passed a variety of gizmos over it and around it. They pushed it gently with a short rod. They finally lifted it with a pair of long metal tongs and headed for the door. Nothing happened. We backed up as the space suit walked, gingerly, to the controlled environment next to the truck. He deposited the box on the metal table. Space suit two slipped a rod under the box lid. He flipped it backward to reveal the tissue paper within. He slowly pushed back the fluffy pinkness and raised it to reveal something. The one with the tongs snatched the object inside the box and held it aloft for all of us to consider. Should we run for cover? It was pink, silky, slinky and barely there. The space suit was holding a thong in one hand and dangling a matching teddy on the end of the rod. I could feel the grins starting. As one, they flipped back their helmets, their gazes left the box and they focused on Lieutenant Jon Stevens.

"Guess we can leave this for you, Lieutenant. It looks a little small, though." The one who had opened the box slid off his space helmet.

"We don't get this good a call very often. Thanks, sweetie." He addressed this to Jon, whose face had shut down into a blank expression. The suit put the offending clothing back, and one of the uniforms came over and picked up the whole thing. He strolled slowly over to Jon and made a show of handing it over, tissue, bow and contents. The suits and uniforms returned to their vehicles. I could hear the giggling.

"Who the hell would send me that?" He growled, stepping back into the hallway.

I was wondering that myself when Lucille stuck her head in the doorway and sang out.

"Is everything okay, Jonny?"

Ah, the light dawns. The bomb squad pulled away from the curb and made its dignified and slow trip, followed by the uniforms in their patrol cars, down the street. Life on Lincoln Avenue would resume its sedate pace. Jon would eventually live down the incident at cop central, but it would take some time.

"I hope the gift works for you. I got one like it and it was just what I needed." Lucille smiled her angelic best.

Jon grunted and closed the door in her face.

He walked over with the now-infamous box. He lifted the offending garments out and held them up. He turned around and looked at me.

"Put it on," he ordered.

Sometimes, it's good to follow orders.

Read on for an excerpt
from Honey Walker's next adventure,

Taxi High

by

S.G. Rogers

When a body fell through the window of my taxi I shrieked like a Hollywood screamer. It was the passenger side and up until 10 seconds ago the body would have been my passenger. Now there was a bullet hole in him and I wasn't sure about his life status. My name is Honey Walker. I drive for Cool Rides Taxi in Northampton, Massachusetts. Questionable bodies are not an everyday event.

He was my first fare of the day. I was running him from town to the Amtrak station in Springfield, about 20 minutes south. He had a paper bag, a bad hair cut, paste white skin and clothes that didn't fit. A red jacket with Bill's Bar BQ and Tropical Fish embroidered across the front was loose over a stained white tee shirt. His pants were electric blue with a gold stripe. The outfit screamed Goodwill. I wondered if he had purposely chosen the red, white and blue color scheme or if it was just at the top of the free box. He leaned in the window to say something. I heard a loud pop and recognized the sound of a gun shot. He slumped and fell forward through the open window.

A cabbie's job is to deliver the client safely, collect the fare money and, hopefully, a tip. Since I hadn't delivered and he hadn't paid, I was 0 for 2, 3 if you consider the tip. I heard another gunshot and a paint chip flew off the hood of my cab. I grabbed the top half of the passenger by his frayed collar and mashed my right foot to the floor. The cab rocketed forward with the bottom half of the passenger flapping against the door like the "Star Spangled Banner" in a hurricane. The safest place I could think of was around the corner so I flew through a stop sign and screeched to a halt in front of the police station. It's a small town.

Two cops standing in front of the station grabbed their radios when they saw my cab with the bottom half of a body hanging out the window. The blood dripping down the side of the cab probably affected their reaction time. One cop pried my fingers off the fare's jacket as an ambulance rolled around the corner.

The EMT yelled "I got a pulse!"

The ambulance went into full scream mode and screeched off with my fare. The other cop removed my white knuckles from the steering wheel. My heart was hammering and I was gulping air like a goldfish on dry land.

In milliseconds I was inside cop central, in an interrogation room. My fare was on his way to the hospital or the morgue. I didn't know which.

The cops seized my taxi. The contents of the almost passenger's paper bag had scattered across the front seat. Lots of prescription pill bottles. He must have had some serious health issues. Now they were either more serious or didn't exist at all.

I sat for at least a million hours waiting for someone to use the interrogation room to interrogate me. There were a few paper cups on the tables and donut crumbs. It was obvious what they usually used it for. When a cop finally came through the door, it was Jon. Police Lieutenant Jon Stevens is a close personal friend. Really, really close. He didn't look happy and I was pretty sure it wasn't because his sex life was lacking.

"We need to talk." He leaned against the door frame with his arms crossed over his chest. He frowned at me. Even unhappy, all six feet of him looked outrageously good. He also looked very much in charge. Right now that meant in charge of me. I'm not good at authority stuff. When pushed I tend to push back. Jon looked ready to push.

At five foot six inches with curly blond hair, blue eyes and a cute turned up nose, I'm the all American girl next door. If you live in the 50s and next door to Ozzie and Harriet.

"All you do is drive a taxi for Christ's sake! This is a small, safe town. How do all these bodies find you?"

"At least I delivered it to your door. And speaking of 'it', did 'it' go to the hospital or the morgue?" My heart rate had slowed to that of a hummingbird so I could talk instead of babble. I was sitting on my hands because they were shaking and I didn't want Jon to see them.

"Hospital. Last I heard he's getting bullets removed from his body."

"So you have some forensic evidence. All those pill bottles must tell you something. And the blood? Maybe you could wash it off my car before I take it back to the Cool Rides garage. Mona's gonna be pissed." Mona is our dispatcher and general guardian of the cars.

"Uh, huh. You ever pick him up before and where were you taking him?"

"No and to the Springfield Amtrak."

"You pick up a lot of people. Any idea where he was headed on the train?"

"No and him I would remember. His hair cut was bad, his clothes didn't fit and he looked like he hadn't seen the sun in a long time."

"He hadn't. He just got out of county."

"County? As in jail county?"

"Uh, huh."

"Then I would guess you knew I hadn't picked him up before."

"Yup."

"You are such a cop." I didn't use the word as a compliment. Jon didn't take the bait. But my hands were finally steady.

"Yup."

"So, can I have my car back?"

"Yeah. We took the bag and bottles and some blood samples. You can run it through the car wash." He grinned. "Good luck with Mona."

Jon knew the Cool Rides staff and he knew Mona would notice the ding in the hood no matter how clean I got the car. And she would be livid.

I snuck the car back to the garage, snatched the hose and scrubbed every inch clean. The missing paint chip on the hood stood out like a zit on a teenager's nose. I knew it would be fixed by the next day. Willy, the majority owner of Cool Rides, and Mona kept the cars immaculate.

I was getting ready to face the wrath of Mona when my cell rang.

"Lucille to the senior center." It was Mona. She was too busy to come out of the office.

"OK. I'm on it." I rolled the hose back, hopped in the car and flew out of the parking lot, happy to put off the inevitable disapproval when Mona saw the tiny little almost non-existent bullet bing in the hood. I'm good at postponing confrontation. Jon would tell Willie anyway, so why aggravate anyone sooner.

When I got to Lucille's house I smelled fresh baked cookies.

"Why, Honey, how nice to see you. How are you?" she said as she slid open her kitchen junk drawer, seeming to forget that she had requested my presence.

"Sort of fine, if you don't count my last customer being shot," I replied.

"Oh, that's nice dear." She absently stared out the window. Lucille's focus was somewhere else and too intense to notice my trivial problems. I decided not to push the subject of my morning disaster.

Sitting down next to the cookies, I watched as she tucked a curl of grey hair behind her ear. She pushed an arthritic finger around the junk drawer, rummaging through cracked rubber bands, unbent paper clips, dried out stamps, a 9mm Glock, ammunition and silencer. She stroked the barrel of the Glock, expertly attached the silencer, shoved bullets into the handle grip and chambered a round. I bit into a freshly baked chocolate chunk macadamia nut cookie, closing my eyes in bliss. Lucille padded to the window. A rabbit hopped across the lawn. It twitched a tiny pink nose sniffing for danger and inched toward the garden. Lucille silently opened the window and steadied her hand on the sill. I glanced at the cookies on the plate in front of me and watched the rabbit lift its white, cotton tail. It left a brown pearl of excrement on the lawn. An incriminating piece of lettuce hung from its mouth. Visions of blood-drenched vegetables danced in my head. I decided not to eat lettuce if Lucille ever offered it, and took another cookie off the plate. Chocolate chip walnut.

"Lucille?"

"Shh."

"Lucille! Don't…"

"Shh!" She repeated with the authority of age and experience.

I took a bite of cookie.

There was a loud pop and a chunk of grass and dirt exploded an inch from rabbit stew. The brown fluff launched itself straight up and hit the grass like a ground ball drilling through the center fielder's stomach. It didn't stop running until it was three houses down.

"Oh, good," Lucille removed the silencer. "That's Marion's yard. She loves animals. It's never good to disturb the neighbors." She smiled, popped the ammo out and returned gun, bullets, and silencer to the drawer.

"So what do you think?" she gestured at the cookie that was half way to my mouth.

"You missed," I gurgled.

"You don't like it?"

"The rabbit."

"Well I didn't want to kill the misguided creature." She looked indignant and swished her flower-print dress as she turned to me. "And I never miss."

She sighed. "Will the cookies help me get lucky with the new geezer wheezer at the senior center?"

"He's gay," I stated.

"Honey, dear, you aren't keeping up. We've had several new arrivals and I need to stake my claim soon or that awful Henrietta will scoop them up. Now focus. The cookies?"

I first met Lucille when I drove her to the airport on her way to scatter her husband's ashes. We got most of him through security and onto the airplane. There was a leak in the box so a little bit of him ended up in the giant ride-around airport vacuum. Some went up the nose of a drug-sniffing beagle. But that was months ago. Lucille was ready to move on with her love life. She looks like Betty White and acts like Clint Eastwood. Sometimes she seems a little vague but I happen to know she has a steel-trap mind and is a great shot with a big gun. Rumor has it she used to work for the FBI.

Lucille pays the fare in cash but she tips in homemade cookies. The object of her cookies and her affection is any unattached male over the age of sixty who knows that oral sex is a two-way street. She lives in a two-family Victorian side by side. Her landlord, who lives on the other side, is the same police Lieutenant Jon Stevens from my recent interview at the cop house.

Jon is four inches taller than me with dark blue eyes that can turn from deep pools of seduction to cop flat way too fast. Lately he's been in a good mood because the city built a new police station. The old building, often referred to as a rat maze, is being turned into a parking garage. So Jon's big blue eyes have been more involved in seduction and less in cop mode. That's good for me.

Lucille rarely worries about who's in charge of her relationships since it is always her. I don't have the same luxury. Jon is an authoritative kind of guy and I'm an anti-authoritative kind of woman.

Lucille tossed her handbag onto the counter. It landed with an ominous thud.

"Let's make sure I have everything we need." Using the pronoun "we" allowed her to add to the bag's contents. She rooted around in the cavernous interior, pulling out two paperbacks. One looked like a steamy romance. The other was a copy of *War and Peace*.

"Excellent examples of fine literature. I never know what kind of mood I might be in." She held up the heavier book. "I've been trying to get through this since I was in high school."

She fished out lipstick, a nail file, and a box of condoms, followed by a purple vibrator.

"Oh, I sincerely hope I need those," she said, pointing to the condoms. "But not that." She slid the vibrator into the kitchen drawer next to the Glock. She pulled out a Swiss army knife with more attachments than my email.

"Not for bridge." She tossed it back to the junk drawer.

"Hmm." She held up dental floss.

I shrugged. "If Julia Roberts needed it in Pretty Woman, why not?"

Lucille dropped it into a pocket and pulled out a roll of toilet paper.

"Is the supply at the senior center inadequate?" I asked.

She smiled and tossed it in the direction of the bathroom. Assorted pens, pencils and note pads were tucked inside and zipped closed. Sun glasses, reading glasses, long-distance glasses, back-up glasses, matches, a flashlight. The last went back into the drawer. Her wallet, checkbook and passport went into a side pocket.

"Now, do you think I need any more defensive weapons? I'll leave the Glock at home, but possibly the brass knuckles? The checkbook in case I lose the bridge game. The passport in case I need to leave the country. And it's a good I.D. More intimidating than a driver's license."

"Lucille, you're going to play bridge for the morning. None of the bridge players are less than seventy years old. Where will you use the condoms? They don't even have beds in the senior center." I ignored the brass knuckles. Seniors are serious about their bridge games.

"Honey, you have no imagination. Haven't you ever done it in a dressing room?" Lucille's eyes misted. "I remember one time in New York. We were in Sax Fifth Avenue…"

"Time to go." I scooped everything into the oversized purse and started out the door. Lucille followed reluctantly, glancing around for something more to cram into the bag.

Going to the senior center probably wouldn't cause any problems between me and Jon. On the rare occasions that our professions overlapped, the results weren't pretty. A taxi is a magnet for people in a hurry. Sometimes they are more anxious to get away from somewhere than to go to somewhere. That may involve police cars in an equal hurry. We get calls from cop central telling us to please not pick up anyone in specific areas. It usually means that the anyone they are talking about is an escaped prisoner or may have just held up the local bank. Small town bank robbers are not known for their long-range plans and they occasionally forget about get-away transportation. More than one has called a cab to take them to and from a robbery. I once got the call from the cops right after I had picked up a scruffy looking character in the vicinity they were worried about. I told them to patch me through to Lt. Jon Stevens, pulled around the corner to the police station and told my fare to get out. There were three uniforms waiting.

But probably not at the senior center. My biggest ambition is to live a life free of drama and filled with music. Taxi driving has the music if I put a disc in the player. Unfortunately it has also had a high level of drama in the two years I've been driving.

Still, before this morning, I hadn't seen Jon for a few days. And one can be a lonely number.

We got to the senior center in five minutes. Lucille got out and heaved her bag with everything that a long-march army would ever want over her shoulder, staggered up the sidewalk and disappeared into the gathering of elders.

I headed back to the Cool Rides garage to see what Mona had on my agenda. Mona is only five feet tall but she guards the taxis like a pit bull and keeps the drivers on target. We always need new drivers. Some drivers, especially guys, have trouble with a female dictator. I went inside to the office so she still hadn't noticed the bullet bing.

"You got a train station, prepaid charge card. Kid's name is Terry." Mona growled and handed me a fare slip.

"I'm on it." I trotted back outside.

The slip gave me name, address, cell phone, time of pick-up and address of drop-off. Pick-up was right away and the train station was twenty minutes down the interstate so I hustled. Exiting the highway sent me through the nicer part of Springfield until I turned up the street to the train station. About a decade ago the station moved from a glorious Grand Central style building to a depressing prefab box. Around the corner is one of the biggest strip clubs in the city. It's a tough part of town. Rumor is that the old station is going to be rebuilt. In the meantime, taxi drivers don't linger.

I pulled into a space near a fire hydrant. There were no cars parked behind me. A big black caddy with tinted windows was three spaces ahead. Most of the train's passengers had hurriedly dispersed. Two people were left. One was a gangly sleepy-eyed teenager with too-big jeans. He was good looking but had a veneer of grime, like he had been living on the street for a while. A big guy in a suit loomed over the kid, blocking the route to my cab. The suit had short legs but looked like his upper body could stop a charging elephant. The teen looked stoned. But he was my fare. I needed to distract the ape and grab my passenger before he turned into a stain on the sidewalk.

"You owe me, fucking low life punk. Those were to sell." The suit was loud and pissed. I lowered both windows on the driver's side. The ape man grabbed the kid, lifting him off the ground. He shoved him against the wall and whispered something in his ear.

"Hey, someone call a cab?" I yelled.

The ape turned and slid his right hand under his jacket. I've watched Lucille practice drawing her weapon at the shooting range. I recognized the move. But he let go of the kid when he went for his gun. In a split second the kid was on the ground and running. Lucky I had lowered the windows because the kid dove through the back one. I felt him hit the seat. The big guy was only two steps behind. He thrust a huge arm through my open window. His other hand waved a gun.

"Shit," I yelped. And it went downhill from there.